The Chief Witness

By Herbert Adams

A Roger Bennion Mystery

Originally published in 1940

The Chief Witness

© 2016 Resurrected Press
www.ResurrectedPress.com

Published by Resurrected Press

This classic book was handcrafted by Resurrected Press. Resurrected Press is dedicated to bringing high quality classic books back to the readers who enjoy them. These are not scanned versions of the originals, but, rather, quality checked and edited books meant to be enjoyed!

Please visit ResurrectedPress.com to view our entire catalogue!

For updates on future releases, LIKE us on Facebook:
http://www.Facebook.com/ResurrectedPress

ISBN 13: 978-1-943403-29-5

Printed in the United States of America

Resurrected Press Books in A. E. Fielding's *The Chief Inspector Pointer Mystery* Series

RESURRECTED PRESS CLASSIC MYSTERY CATALOGUE

Journeys into Mystery
Travel and Mystery in a More Elegant Time

The Edwardian Detectives
Literary Sleuths of the Edwardian Era

Gems of Mystery
Lost Jewels from a More Elegant Age

Anne Austin
One Drop of Blood
The Black Pigeon
Murder at Bridge
Murder Backstairs

E. C. Bentley
Trent's Last Case: The Woman in Black

Ernest Bramah
Max Carrados Resurrected:
The Detective Stories of Max Carrados

Agatha Christie
The Secret Adversary
The Mysterious Affair at Styles

Octavus Roy Cohen
Midnight

Freeman Wills Croft
The Ponson Case
The Pit Prop Syndicate

The Uttermost Farthing: A Savant's Vendetta

Arthur Griffiths
The Passenger From Calais
The Rome Express

Fergus Hume
The Mystery of a Hansom Cab
The Green Mummy
The Silent House
The Secret Passage

Edgar Jepson
The Loudwater Mystery

A. E. W. Mason
At the Villa Rose

A. A. Milne
The Red House Mystery

Baroness Emma Orczy
The Old Man in the Corner

Edgar Allan Poe
The Detective Stories of Edgar Allan Poe

Arthur J. Rees
The Hampstead Mystery
The Shrieking Pit
The Hand In The Dark
The Moon Rock
The Mystery of the Downs

Mary Roberts Rinehart
Sight Unseen and The Confession

Dorothy L. Sayers

Whose Body?

Sir William Magnay
The Hunt Ball Mystery

Mabel and Paul Thorne
The Sheridan Road Mystery

Louis Tracy
The Strange Case of Mortimer Fenley
The Albert Gate Mystery
The Bartlett Mystery
The Postmaster's Daughter
The House of Peril
The Sandling Case: What Would You Have Done?

Charles Edmonds Walk
The Paternoster Ruby

John R. Watson
The Mystery of the Downs
The Hampstead Mystery

Edgar Wallace
The Daffodil Mystery
The Crimson Circle

Carolyn Wells
Vicky Van
The Man Who Fell Through the Earth
In the Onyx Lobby
Raspberry Jam
The Clue
The Room with the Tassels
The Vanishing of Betty Varian
The Mystery Girl
The White Alley
The Curved Blades

Anybody but Anne
The Bride of a Moment
Faulkner's Folly
The Diamond Pin
The Gold Bag
The Mystery of the Sycamore
The Come Back

Raoul Whitfield
Death in a Bowl

And much more!
Visit ResurrectedPress.com
for our complete catalogue

FOREWORD

Herbert Adams was one of the writers who came out of the period between the two world wars which has been called "The Golden Age of British Detective Fiction." It was a period during which the mystery novel was enormously popular. Indeed, nearly a quarter of all fiction published in Britain during this period were mysteries. Adams' first mystery, The *Secret of Bogey House* was published in 1924, and in the thirty years following, he would go on to write over fifty more.

Unlike many of the mystery writers of the period who were in their twenties and thirties when they started writing, Adams was fifty when *The Secret of Bogey House* came out. He was part of that late Victorian middle class that had seen their world change so drastically, from horses and steam locomotives to radio and aeroplanes. With the upheavals in economics and politics that affected their lives, this class struggled to retain the way of life that they had grown up expecting. It is no wonder that they turned to mysteries for an escape.

Murder in this period, at least in fiction, tended to be neither brutal or random. While there were British authors who wrote about gangsters in the American style, for most of them crime was more genteel. Cleverness and innovation in the means of murder were highly prized, and a certain amount of humor was always to be appreciated. Adams certainly fit that mold. His murders often took place at country homes or that most British of institutions, the golf course. The puzzle element is preeminent, and violence is at a minimum and usually off stage.

While Adams wrote a few stand alone mysteries, his early mysteries featured London lawyer Jimmie Haswell. In his later mysteries, he favored Roger Bennion, an avid golfer, as his amateur sleuth, though Roger often worked in conjunction with Inspector Goff of Scotland Yard.

The Chief Witness is one of the Roger Bennion mysteries. It begins with a conversation about coincidence. This, of course, is followed by the apparent suicides of two brothers at exactly eleven o'clock. The time of death is established by a fallen clock in one case, and a smashed watch in the other, both of which stopped at the exact instance. There seemed to be no reason for either brother to kill himself, one was a prominent lawyer, the other a partner in a successful accountancy, and they lived miles apart from each other. Neither Goff or Bennion place much faith in coincidence, and the novel revolves around their efforts first to prove that it was murder, and then to prove the innocence of the man who is the leading suspect.

In the three quarters of a century since it was published, Herbert Adams has faded into obscurity, as have so many of the mystery writers of the period, yet his works are still entertaining to read. It is with pleasure that Resurrected Press presents this new edition of *The Chief Witness.*

About the Cover
The cover includes elements of the original hardcover dustjacket.

About the Author
Herbert Adams (1874-1958) was an English author of over fifty mystery novels. Though his first novel, *A Virtue of Necessity*, was published in 1899, it wasn't until the 1920's that his career as a mystery writer took off with a series of books featuring the London lawyer Jimmie Haswell. This was followed by a second series featuring Roger Bennion, a golfer an amateur detective. Many of the books in this series were centered around a golfing theme. Adams also wrote a number of non-series mysteries. In addition he wrote two mysteries, a number

of short stories, and humorous verse using the pseudonym Jonathan Gray

Greg Fowlkes
Editor-In-Chief
Resurrected Press
www.ResurrectedPress.

TABLE OF CONTENTS

I. COINCIDENCE

"I WONDER," said Sir Christopher Bennion, "how many of us really become what in our youths we hoped to be? Very few, I imagine."

"You could not have a male population entirely of railway guards and airmen," his son Roger remarked.

"I was not referring to nursery fancies," replied the father, "but to a young man's ideas when he begins to take life seriously."

"I always wanted to be a millionaire-philanthropist," said Gordon Lisle. "I became a journalist. The next best thing, of course."

"Better," said Roger. "Your millionaire-philanthropist can only give away what he himself possesses. The journalist can dispose of what everyone owns anywhere."

"What is your experience, Inspector Goff?" asked the baronet, turning to the fourth of the party, a burly clean-shaven, full-faced man who was smoking a big pipe and enjoying his drink.

"Well, Sir Christopher," he replied, removing his pipe from his mouth, "if few men become what they hoped to be, I am an exception. My father was a policeman; I always wanted to be a policeman; I am a policeman."

"Born with a whistle in his mouth," murmured Roger, "and protesting loudly when his mother diluted the bottle with more than the statutory proportion of water."

The others laughed. It is always funny to picture a very big man as a baby. Actually they had met together in Goff's honour. Sir Christopher, knowing that his son had worked with the eminent detective in several important cases, had expressed a desire to meet him. So Roger had arranged the little party at his Sloane Street flat, asking Gordon Lisle to complete the number. Lisle, a fair-haired young fellow of about his own age, was the "crime editor" on a popular Sunday newspaper. It was up to him to see that its readers got the fullest possible details of all the nastiest happenings of the week, and he did his job well. He and Goff had met before, though never perhaps on such amicable terms.

"A policeman's life," Sir Christopher said, "must offer more interest and variety than most."

"I don't know," drawled Lisle, "one drunk and disorderly must be very like another, and even smelling motorists' breath to swear they are incapable of driving must pall after a time."

"There is a lot of routine work in the ranks," said Goff, unruffled, "but I have no complaint on that score."

"Murder, arson, robbery, treason, alien spies and the I.R.A.," murmured Roger. "Sheer joy all the time."

"The detection of crime," observed Sir Christopher, "is largely a matter of hard work and persistence, we all know that. But how often does coincidence come into it?"

"Rather depends, sir, what you mean by coincidence," said the inspector.

"Shrewdly put," nodded Lisle.

"Coincidence, according to Euclid," said Roger, "is falling together, or occupying the same space. He taught us how to prove it, but there I generally stuck."

"I was using the word," explained Sir Christopher, "in the customary sense, implying the unexpected. A combination of events that could not be foreseen or counted on."

"Life is made up of coincidence," Lisle declared. "John Brown on holiday stays at the same boarding house as Janet Smith, and Janet Smith becomes Mrs. Brown and the mother of the little Browns, if any. Had John Brown gone elsewhere he would have married Ethel Jones, while Janet would have become Mrs. Robinson. In after years Mrs. Robinson might meet Mrs. Brown and say, if only she realised it, 'What a queer coincidence! If your husband had gone to Bella Vista and mine to Ocean View, instead of the other way about, I should be the mother of your children!'"

"Circumstances shape our lives," agreed Sir Christopher, "but that is hardly what I meant. If this Mrs. Brown had some valuable diamonds and left her safe unlocked for the first time on the very night a burglar visited her, that I should call a very unfortunate coincidence."

"I should enquire about the insurance policy," grunted Goff, relighting his pipe.

"Meaning you do not believe in coincidence?" Roger asked.

"Not quite that, but a burglary in such circumstances generally means an inside job. Someone sees the open safe and fakes a fictitious entry."

"But suppose the burglary is genuine," said Lisle, "and while searching for something else you come across part of the loot and so catch the criminal?"

"That happens, but if we want a thing there are a thousand men up and down the land on the lookout for it. It is not surprising if one of them finds it, even if he was looking for something else at the time."

"But coincidences do occur," said Roger. "The other day I saw car JT 6001 standing next to car TJ 6001. The owners were complete strangers; I was curious enough to ask. The odds against such a thing must be enormous."

"We are told it is billions to one against a card-player being dealt a complete suit," Lisle said, "but we read about it fairly frequently."

"The most curious coincidence I ever experienced," remarked Sir Christopher, "happened before I was married. I was staying at a hotel and was told I was wanted on the telephone. I went, and a lady's voice said, 'Is that you, Chris?' 'It is,' I replied, 'who are you?' 'Julia, your sister,' was the answer. 'I think you must want someone else,' I said. 'But you are Christopher Bennion? I am Julia.' The weird thing was that I had had a sister

Julia, and had attended her funeral only a few weeks before. It gave me quite a shock."

"Was it a badly-timed joke, sir?" asked Lisle.

"No. It was all perfectly genuine. Another Christopher Bennion had been at the hotel a few days previously, and his sister Julia had rung up to see if he was still there. Not common names, but it happened."

"The oddest case I know of," said Roger, "and I believe it is well authenticated, was of three men, a Canadian, a New Zealander and an Englishman, who were in hospital together in 1918 and became very good friends. Twenty years afterwards the Canadian brought his wife to London for the first time, and on the night of their arrival, sitting at the next table in a restaurant, was the New Zealander, who had brought his wife, also for the first time on a similar visit. They decided to go somewhere together and the commissionaire who called a taxi for them was their old friend the Englishman."

"I hope they took him with them," said Lisle.

"They certainly arranged a meeting."

"I can cap that," Goff observed. "One of our fellows was on holiday at Brighton, and the photographer who snaps you as you pass along the front took a picture of him and handed him a card saying where it would be on view. He had vanity enough to go along the next day to see what he looked like. There was a display board with dozens of them, and close to his photograph was one of a man we had badly wanted for some time. We had no idea where he was, but that snap put us on the trail and he was arrested the same night. An embezzlement case. He got five years."

"That shows I was right," said Sir Christopher. "Coincidence catches criminals in fact as well as in fiction."

"I am not denying that, sir. I only say if we waited for coincidences a lot of criminals would escape."

The talk went on for a long time, and each had more stories to tell. At last Sir Christopher decided he must be going, and that was the signal for the others also to depart. Roger went down to see them off.

"Still raining," said Lisle. "What a summer!"

The baronet offered him and Goff a lift in his spacious car, which was gladly accepted.

When he returned to his room, Roger saw that Goff had forgotten his pipe. A well-bitten briar, left on the little table beside an empty glass.

A very trivial thing. But, had Goff taken that pipe with him, a curious crime would never have been cleared up and an innocent man might have hanged.

II. IN DEATH TOGETHER

Inspector Gorff was frowning over the usual pile of official papers when Roger called on him the next morning at Scotland Yard.

"Surprised you did not miss it," the visitor said, handing over the pipe.

"I did, when I got home," the detective replied. "I was pretty sure I had left it at your place, but I might of course have dropped it."

"An easy scent to follow! It is time you had a new one."

"Thanks for bringing it. I don't like new pipes."

He spoke rather shortly and Roger turned to go, not wanting to interrupt the work of a busy man. Goff, however, stopped him.

"We were talking last night about coincidences. If two men, brothers, committed suicide in almost identical circumstances, and at precisely the same moment, half a mile apart—what would you call that?"

"If it was by agreement, I suppose I should call it insanity. If they did it entirely independently of one another, it would be the queerest coincidence on record."

Goff grunted in his characteristic way and frowned again at the paper on his desk.

"Did it happen?" Roger asked.

"It did. At two minutes to eleven last night. Just when we were talking of such things."

"People of position?"

"An apparently well-to-do solicitor and an apparently equally well-to-do accountant."

"Generally hard-headed people," said Roger; "not the suicide type. But if they were jointly concerned in some financial affair that failed, it might account for it."

"I am awaiting a reply to enquiries as to their finances, then I am going to look into things. It all seems simple enough, but the Chief is not satisfied. Like to come with me?"

"I would," Roger replied. "To be in on such a case from the start should be very instructive, however straightforward it might be. May I ask who the people are?"

"The solicitor is Alexander Curtis, of Morant and Curtis of Lincoln's Inn. Age about fifty. He lived in a service flat in Hans Avenue, not far from Sloane Street, with his wife. No children. The body was found at seven this morning by a maid who came in to tidy up the living room."

"The wife was away?"

"No. But she says she knew nothing about it. Greatly shocked, of course. The man was shot in the head and the revolver was at his feet."

"Finger-prints in order, I suppose?"

"Being verified."

"Any sort of letter of farewell or explanation?"

"Not in either case," replied Goff, "so far as is at present known."

"Curious. How was the time fixed?"

"In falling he apparently knocked over a clock that stands on his desk and it stopped at two minutes to eleven. The doctor who was called directly the body was found gave that time as about right."

"You may find he has been ill or depressed," said Roger. "What about the other case?"

"Frederick Curtis, practising as an accountant in London Wall. A widower, living with his daughter Delia in a small house in Egerton Square, off the Brompton Road. A year or two younger than his brother Alexander.

Shot in the head in precisely the same way at two minutes to eleven."

"Did he also knock a clock over?" asked Roger.

"No. When he fell he broke the glass of his wristwatch, and that put it out of action. Doctor certifies the time of death as correct."

"When was this body found?"

"The story there is a bit different. Delia, the daughter, rather a gay young person, came in from a night club or a bottle party or something of the sort, with a bunch of her friends at about three a.m. She apparently promised them another drink and went to her father's room to get it, thinking he would have gone to bed. She discovered the body and gave the alarm."

"In each case the men were at home alone?"

"Apparently."

"And no one heard a shot?"

"Not so far as we know. But my enquiries have not yet begun. We have just had the preliminary reports."

"It may prove simple enough," said Roger, "when you learn what sort of men they were. I should look for prearrangement rather than coincidence. For one man to die in such a way, with no note of explanation or farewell, would be curious; but for two to do it at the same moment seems hardly credible, unless they were faced by some common disaster. You are sure Frederick was a year or two younger than Alexander?"

"That is my information. Why?"

"One hears odd stories of twins who fall ill together and share each other's sensations in a remarkable way, although it would be a very extreme case of telepathy for one to commit suicide because the other was doing so—except of course by previous agreement. But as the Curtis brothers are not twins you must look for something less fantastic."

At that moment the telephone bell sounded, and Goff listened with brief interjections to a fairly long statement.

"That's that," he muttered, replacing the receiver. "From enquiries at the banks and business houses of both the men their affairs are perfectly in order, and, so far as is known, there is no financial difficulty in either case."

"Insanity in the family?" asked Roger.

"That remains to be seen. We had better get going."

Inspector Goff decided to call first on the widow of the solicitor, Alexander Curtis. The journey did not take long and neither he nor Roger said much on the way. There were probably many questions that each of them could have asked, but it would be time enough for that when they faced those who might be able to answer them.

The block of service flats was at the corner of Hans Avenue and close to Sloane Square. A noisy position, but a very convenient one for a man with an office in Lincoln's Inn. Roger noted that the lift was automatic. They shot swiftly up to the top floor, on which was the flat for which they were bound.

Goff pressed the bell and the door was opened by a policeman in uniform, who saluted on seeing him.

"Who is here?" asked the inspector.

"Sergeant Queen, sir. Waiting for you. The others have gone."

"Mrs. Curtis in?"

"Yes, sir. In her bedroom."

Roger followed Goff into the sitting-room from which the body had not yet been removed. Sergeant Queen, a thin, alert-looking man, spoke in a subdued tone of voice.

"The photographers and the finger-print men have finished. They have taken the gun to test it. Otherwise nothing has been disturbed."

It was a comfortably furnished room that apparently served as a study as well as a general sitting-room. A costly Persian carpet, some well-padded easy chairs, and, by the window, a flat-topped dark oak desk with a leather writing chair were its most notable appointments. The body of the dead man lay on the floor near the desk. A few feet away was a small gilt clock. It was face upwards and the hands still pointed to two minutes to eleven.

Goff bent over the body and looked at the wound in the side of the head near the right temple.

"Gun held close to head," he muttered. "Must have been standing up, or he would have remained in the chair."

"Clock tested for finger-prints?" asked Roger.

"Not yet, sir," Queen replied. "We thought if we moved it, it might start going again. We left it for Inspector Goff to see."

"Do you know where on the desk it stood?"

"No, sir. Mrs. Curtis may be able to tell us that."

Goff made a careful examination of all the things that he thought might be of interest. He noted that the few papers on the desk were not disordered and that an opened book, a historical novel, lay face downwards as though the user of the room had recently been reading it.

"What is there about Charles II and his ladies that should make a man put the book down and shoot himself?" Roger enquired.

No one was prepared with a reply, and Goff, having finished his examination, asked: "Is there another sitting-room?"

"Yes, sir," said Queen. "The place where they eat."

"I will see Mrs. Curtis there."

III. THE WIDOW

It would be unjust to judge any woman's looks by her appearance a few hours after she had suddenly heard of her husband's suicide.

Helen Curtis was seated in a low chair when they entered her room, and she made a motion to them to sit down. She was about forty years of age. As a girl she had undoubtedly been attractive, with that fair-haired type of prettiness that comes from a fresh colour and an animated expression. She had coarsened with the passing years, and her blue eyes were hard. She seemed shocked at the tragedy that had befallen her, yet there was no signs of deep personal grief.

"This is a very distressing business," Goff began in his most soothing manner, "but I am sure you will help me in every way you can."

"Of course I will," she said. Her voice was low and not unpleasing.

"How long have you and your husband lived here?"

"About four years. We have a cottage in Gloucestershire as well."

"Had your husband been in good health lately?"

"He had not complained. His digestion was a little troublesome sometimes."

"He had not been depressed?"

"Not that I was aware of."

There was little sympathy in her tone. Roger, who was listening to all that was said, formed the impression that she and her husband had not got on too well together. Probably Goff thought the same. He led up to it with his usual tact.

"What is the accommodation of this flat?"

"You can see over it if you like."

"I will, but perhaps you would describe it to me."

"It is really two flats thrown into one. The whole of the floor. So there are two bedrooms, two sitting-rooms and two bath rooms."

"This is the dining-room?"

In the modern way it was not a room designed solely for meals. There was a table against the wall that folded into a very small space and there were four chairs of a suitable design to go with it, but, for the rest, the furnishing was that of a lady's sitting-room. It had a low couch, padded seats and small tables with a superfluity of ornaments.

"If we have meals up here," Mrs. Curtis said in reply to his question.

"Is that unusual?"

"There is a restaurant downstairs, and we were out a good deal."

"What did you do last night?"

For a moment the woman hesitated. Then she spoke more quickly.

"My husband brought home two tickets for the theatre, which his partner Mr. Morant had given him. He did not wish to go, so I telephoned to my sister to meet me and have some dinner first. We went to the Trocadero because that is near the theatre. Afterwards I came home alone."

"Your husband seemed in normal health and spirits when you left him?"

"I—I think so."

"He had his dinner up here, or in the restaurant?"

"I don't know. When he was alone he generally had something up here."

"To what theatre did you go?"

"To the Cardinal. It was the second night of a new play. I think Mr. Morant, or clients of his, have an interest in it."

"At what time did you get home?"

"I do not know exactly. Plays generally end about eleven. Mr. Morant spoke to me before I went out and asked me what I thought of it. I was talking to him for a little time. I suppose I was back between half-past eleven and twelve."

"I notice it is an automatic lift. You brought yourself up and went straight to your room?"

"That is so."

"You and your husband have separate rooms?"

"We have."

"Did you look into his room, or his bedroom?"

"I did not. I thought he would have gone to bed and did not wish to disturb him."

"Would that be usual when you had been out?"

"Quite usual," she said in the same hard tone.

"When did you first know what had happened?"

"When the maid came up this morning to straighten the rooms. She saw—she saw him, and she told me."

"Thank you, Mrs. Curtis. Can you account in any way for your husband shooting himself?"

"I cannot."

"Had he ever threatened to do such a thing?"

"Never. He seemed to enjoy life, in his own way." There was bitterness in her tone and Goff paused a moment before he went on again.

"Was he expecting any visitors last evening?"

"He did not say so."

"If he had any, I suppose they would come up in the lift as you did, and he would admit them?"

"Unless they rang for the porter to bring them up."

"I did not see a porter," said Goff.

"You would not, unless you rang for him."

"So visitors might come and go without being seen?"

"Most likely."

"You have of course heard that his brother, Mr. Frederick Curtis, also shot himself at apparently the same time last night?"

"Mr. Morant told me so."

"When did he tell you?"

"He telephoned a little before you came here. He said you had sent someone to the office who had told him about it. He was very kind. He said he would come round as soon as he could, in case he could be of any help."

"I see. Were the two brothers, your husband and Frederick, on good terms?"

"Very."

"Had they many interests in common?"

"How do you mean? They both played golf, and they had business together."

"What I mean is, could some common disaster or disappointment have led them both to end their lives in that way, and at the same time?"

"I cannot account for it anyhow else. But I have no idea what the disaster could have been. Mr. Morant told me there was no trouble of that kind. He could not explain it at all."

Her emotionless way of speaking was really remarkable. Roger found himself wondering whether she did not care, or whether she restrained herself with a strong will-power that would sooner or later fail her.

"You have no children?" asked Goff.

"No."

"Had your husband any other relations besides Frederick and Frederick's daughter?"

"There is another brother, Marmaduke. He is on the Stock Exchange."

"The Stock Exchange? Might the brothers have speculated through him?"

"I never heard of it. I do not like Marmaduke."

Her likes were of no particular moment and it did not seem that Goff could get much further.

"Frederick could have come here last night," he said, as though thinking aloud, "or they might have telephoned one another. We can enquire about the calls." Then he asked the name and address of the sister with whom Mrs. Curtis had spent the evening.

"Mrs. Farr, of Colston Court, Kensington," was the reply.

"Were you and your husband on good terms?" asked Goff bluntly.

Mrs. Curtis did not seem to resent the enquiry. She shrugged her shoulders. "As good terms as many other people."

As Goff had apparently nothing more to ask, Roger enquired if he might put a question.

"Your husband was a studious man, Mrs. Curtis?" he said pleasantly.

"He read a good deal," she replied. "Though he had other amusements."

"Was he of what I would call fixed habits?"

"What do you mean?" She looked at him as though wondering what lay behind the question.

"Some of us, and I believe it becomes more pronounced as we grow older, like to have the things we use always in the same place. Pipes, slippers, papers, just where we know we shall find them."

"Oh, yes, he was very much that way."

"He would wish the things on his desk always arranged the same—the inkpot, the ash-tray, the reading lamp, and so on?"

"Yes. He was quite fussy about it."

"Where did his little clock generally stand?"

"His clock? At the back of his desk, to the left."

"Always there?"

"I never remember seeing it anywhere else."

"If he was standing in front of his desk when he shot himself, could he have knocked over the clock?"

She stared at him, and some of the colour faded from her cheeks.

"I do not quite understand," she muttered.

"Unless he fell across the desk," said Roger gently, "he could not have reached the clock. From the position in which he was found, and the orderly condition of his papers, I do not think he fell across the desk."

"Perhaps—perhaps I was wrong. The clock was not always at the back of the desk."

"Had you ever known it stand anywhere else?"

"I—I think I had."

"You told Inspector Goff that you thought your husband enjoyed life in his own way. What exactly did you mean?"

She stared at him for some moments.

"I meant he liked books and that sort of thing."

"But you said he had other amusements?"

"No one can be reading all the time."

Before Roger could say any more the constable entered the room to inform his superior officer that a Mr. Morant had called and was wishing to see Mrs. Curtis.

"Bring him in," said Goff.

IV. THE PARTNER

VICTOR Morant, partner of the late Alexander Curtis, was a striking-looking man in the mid-fifties. His silver-white hair contrasted vividly with a smooth, fresh complexion, and strong black brows. He was slightly built, of barely medium height, but his was a personality not to be overlooked. He was obviously a man who knew his own mind and acted promptly in the way he saw right. He was neatly dressed with a black jacket and dark striped trousers.

When he entered the room he went straight to Mrs. Curtis and took her hand in both of his.

"You know how distressed I am," he said simply. "Please rely on me to help you in every way I can. I take it these gentlemen represent the police?"

"They do," she said.

She did not appear to return his greeting with any particular warmth. Roger's impression was that the offer to help her was from sympathy and a sense of duty, not because of any strong friendship between them.

Goff introduced himself and said he had intended to call on Mr. Morant at his office.

"Certainly," the solicitor said. "Or if you prefer it, and Mrs. Curtis permits, I can answer any questions now."

"It would save time," said Goff.

"Have you asked Mrs. Curtis all you wish to know from her?"

"For the time being," the Inspector replied.

"Then might I suggest she be allowed to retire to her room? We do not wish to cause her unnecessary distress."

"It might be best," said Goff.

Without a word Mrs. Curtis left them. She moved slowly, and Roger, who opened the door for her, thought

she would have preferred to stay, to hear what was said.
But she could hardly ask to be allowed to do so.

"I suppose you knew both the Curtis brothers very
well?" Goff began.

"I knew Alexander very well indeed. He was my
partner for twenty years. We started together. I need
hardly say what a gap in my life his death will mean.
With his brother Frederick I was not so intimate, though
we met fairly frequently."

"Can you in any way account for their killing
themselves last night?"

"Indeed I cannot. When one of your men called this
morning and told me about it, I could hardly believe him.
It seemed incredible, impossible. I am still bewildered
and find it hard to adjust my thoughts to it."

He showed more emotion than the widow had done.
Partners for a number of years may become almost more
than brothers.

"Was Alexander Curtis subject to fits of depression?"

Morant considered the question for some moments
before he replied.

"I do not think his private, or business affairs
depressed him. He was perhaps inclined to take world
affairs too seriously."

"How do you mean?"

"He regarded war as inevitable and he saw in it the
destruction of our civilisation. He visualised all too
clearly the suffering and desolation it would entail.
Alternatively, if by some miracle war could be avoided, he
was convinced that over-taxation and unemployment
must bring about revolution and economic ruin."

"He was a shrewd business man?" asked Goff.

"Most decidedly."

"Yet you say these fears for the future led him to
suicide?"

"On the contrary," said Mr. Morant. "These things
weighed on him very much, yet I find it impossible to
persuade myself they could account for so desperate an

act. We often discussed public affairs, but unfortunately I could never get him to adopt my views as to the real remedy for our troubles."

"What is your remedy?" Roger enquired.

"Are you asking that as a policeman?"

"I am not a policeman," said Roger. "I have no official standing. I want to help Inspector Goff if I can."

"Mr. Roger Bennion," said Goff tersely.

Morant nodded. "Not by any chance related to Sir Christopher Bennion?" he asked.

"My father."

"Then I am delighted to meet you," the solicitor declared warmly. "I have met Sir Christopher and have a great respect for him. He might not approve of what you call my remedy, but it can be given in two words—capital levy. Not a new idea. It has been talked about, but never tried here. I do not think there will be a war but, whether there is or not, our financial position can only be remedied by the most drastic action. Our colossal debts must be wiped out by compulsory contribution from all classes according to their means. It will be painful, as all severe operations are painful. I shall be hit, as your father and every well-to-do person will be hit. But our generation, must suffer if we are to survive. I am standing for Parliament as an independent candidate and that is my battle cry."

He stopped abruptly and turned to Goff with something of a smile.

"I am sorry, Inspector. This young man started me on my pet subject. I must not waste your time with it. Except for despondency as to the future, I should say Alexander Curtis was in every way a normal hard-headed man."

"Did he take an active part in politics?" asked the Inspector.

"No. He read a lot and, unluckily, he seemed always ready to believe the worst."

"His own affairs were in order?"

"Undoubtedly. I think it will prove he died a wealthy man."

"Was his home life happy?"

Morant hesitated.

"I should say he and Mrs. Curtis understood one another. I would prefer to leave it at that."

"How long had they been married?"

"About ten years."

"Had he been married before?"

"No."

"He was at his office yesterday as usual?"

"Yes. I was out most of the day and did not see him until the late afternoon. Then I went to his room and offered him some tickets for the theatre for the evening."

"Did he accept them?"

"I suggested he should take his wife, but she came without him. I saw her when the show was over and was rather disappointed he was not there, as I had a special reason for asking him to go. But that will not interest you."

"It might," said Goff, "if we knew why he did not do so."

"It was a new play, Labour of Love, at the Cardinal Theatre. The night before was the first night, and it was not very well received. I have an interest in it, and had spent a good deal of the day with the principals and other parties concerned suggesting cuts and improvements. I wanted to get my partner's view of it; not as a theatrical expert but as that of an ordinary intelligent playgoer. So I was disappointed when Mrs. Curtis came without him."

"Was she alone?" asked Roger.

"I do not think she was, but I really did not notice her companion."

"Did her opinion interest you?"

"Not so much as her husband's would have done."

"Except for this sort of feeling of bad times ahead," said Goff, "you can suggest no reason for your partner ending his life?"

"None whatever," Morant replied, "and I do not want you to think I regard that as having been acute enough to account for it. It is just that I cannot imagine anything else."

"Then as to Frederick, the brother. I have not been into that very fully yet, but is there anything you can tell me about him? When did you last see him?"

"Two days ago he called at our office and I saw him and Alexander together. I should have said he was perfectly normal. He was a reserved man, especially since his wife died. Our young people knew one another better than he and I did."

"What young people?"

"He has a daughter, Delia," explained Morant, "and I have a niece, Margot Watney, who lives with me. Delia and Margot are great friends. Frederick Curtis also has a nephew—I suppose I must say he had a nephew—Wilfrid Mounsey. The two girls and Wilfrid are, I believe, very friendly, and they have a group of other young people round them. They like to rush about together in the modern way, but it is all innocent enough. A lot of noise, but no mischief."

"Another brother, isn't there?" asked Goff. "You know him?"

"Marmaduke, the youngest of the three. He is on the Stock Exchange. I meet him occasionally, but I do not know him as well as I knew his brothers."

"Is there any taint of insanity in the family? Has Marmaduke ever shown any queer kinks?"

"I have never heard any suggestions of insanity," said Morant, "and Marmaduke certainly never displayed it. The three brothers, though not unlike in appearance, were curiously dissimilar in character. Alexander, my partner, I should describe as of the domesticated type. He was a keen lawyer, of course, but when his work was done he liked a quiet home life. If there was any friction at all between him and his wife it would have been on that account; she desiring to enjoy society in a way that did not appeal to him. He liked his evenings at home; she did not. I often thought they would have been happier if they had had children."

"So they were not happy?" said Goff.

"Happiness is a relative term. There are many stages between perfect contentment and continuous quarrels. He was not a quarrelsome man."

"Well—Frederick?"

"I should call him austere," Morant replied. "He was deeply religious and never joined in his young people's fun. While not forbidding it, he often showed his disapproval. That, at least, is the impression my niece has given me. His wife died a few years ago, as I told you. Since then he became more of a recluse."

"Would that account for his suicide?"

Morant made a gesture expressive of uncertainty.

"I cannot account for it in any other way," he said. "I some times tried to interest both him and Alexander in other things. I like to live every moment of the day—my work, the theatre and politics—but they had few outside interests."

"The surviving brother, you say, is a different sort of man?"

"You will, no doubt, see Marmaduke and judge of him for yourself," Morant replied. "If we had business on the Stock Exchange we sent it to him, just as we sent accountancy work to Frederick. He is more assertive than his brothers. Sometimes, perhaps, a little too assertive. If they were home lovers, he was not. But I do not think there is any point in my discussing him. He will, of course, be able to tell you more of his brothers than I can."

There were a few further questions, but although Morant spoke freely he was unable to throw any real light on the twofold mystery.

"One suicide," said Goff at last, "might be explicable, but for two brothers to kill themselves apparently at the same moment, and for no known reason, is something new in my experience. There must be some explanation for it."

"It baffles me completely," said Morant. "Apart from the distress it causes me, I should be happier if I could in some way account for it. I hope your enquiries may have such success as is possible. You may rely on me for any assistance in my power."

As he was remaining to see Mrs. Curtis, Goff and Roger decided to visit the other house of tragedy.

"I am interested in your scheme for curing our social ills," Roger said as they parted. "Some day I would like to hear more of it."

"Certainly, my boy, certainly. You must come to one of my meetings. I would like you to meet my niece."

V. THE DAUGHTER

EGERTON SQUARE IS not a square; it has only two
sides. Its houses do not face a garden; they back on one. A
site once occupied by stables and workmen's cottages had
been cleared and two rows of non-basement residences
erected upon it, with a strip of garden between them.
Their accommodation is small but their price high. They
combine the last word in labour-saving convenience with
an attempt at "old-world" charm. They are seldom empty.

On arriving at No. 3, where Frederick Curtis had
lived, Inspector Goff, Roger Bennion and Sergeant Queen
found officers in possession waiting for them. The tragedy
there had been discovered during the night and, although
it had been duly reported, it is probable it would not have
fallen to the chief-inspector to investigate it had it not
been for the death of the brother, of which the news was
received some hours later.

Morant had described Frederick Curtis as an austere
man. The room in which he worked, or amused himself,
and in which he had died, was a pleasant one. It had
glass doors opening on to a narrow tiled portico which,
with two steps, led into the garden. It should have been
quiet, but the rumble of traffic never quite ceased.

The furnishing of the room was simple, though not
severely so. There was indeed a distinct air of comfort
about it. A finely polished mahogany desk, a writing chair
in padded leather, two deeply cushioned easy-chairs,
shelves with a number of serious books—these were the
first things to strike the eye. Or they would have been
were it not for the stiffened body that lay on the thick
Turkey carpet close to the desk.

"We were rung up soon after 3 a.m.," said Inspector
Groves from the local station, "and came round at once.

The doctor came too. It seemed simple enough, and we arranged for the ambulance to call about 9 o'clock. Then news came through of the other case, so we left things as they were."

"Quite right," said Goff, and for some while he devoted himself to his grim duties.

The wound was in much the same place as in the case of the brother, above the ear, but it was on the other side of the head.

"Shot on the left side!" exclaimed Goff.

"Yes, sir. He was a left-handed man. His daughter said so, but I made sure of it. He has a bag of golf clubs in the hall and they are left-handed clubs. That seemed to make it pretty certain."

Goff did not reply. He was staring at the revolver which lay close to the body, and at the dead man's hand extended palm downwards on the carpet.

"Finger-prints taken?"

"Not yet, sir. Expecting them now."

"Time fixed by this?'"

Goff pointed to the wrist-watch, the glass of which was badly broken.

"Yes, sir. Stopped at two minutes to eleven. The daughter said it had always kept good time."

"Were those glass doors open or shut?" asked Roger Bennion, pointing to the way to the garden.

He was standing still, but his eyes had been scanning every object in the room. He had scrutinised the desk and had bent over the carpet where the body lay.

"Shut when we got here," Groves replied, "but not locked or bolted."

"Would that be usual?"

"I have not questioned the young lady about it."

"Find out if she can see me," said Goff. "I suppose there is another room?"

There was a room in the front, facing the street, and in it not one, but two young ladies were waiting for them.

"Miss Curtis?" questioned Goff.

"I am Delia Curtis," said the taller of the two. She was fair, with little make-up, and she looked as though she had been crying. "This is my friend, Miss Watney."

"Margot Watney?" asked Roger, looking with some interest at the shorter dark girl, who was decidedly pretty. Both she and Delia might have been about twenty years of age.

"How did you know that?" she demanded, her brown eyes showing her surprise.

"We have just seen your uncle, Mr. Morant. He told us you were Miss Curtis's friend."

"I can tell you almost as much as she can," said Margot. "I was with her last night when—when she came home. It was ghastly for her, so I hope you will let me do most of the talking."

She was a brisk young woman and, like her uncle, seemed to know her own mind.

"I think Miss Curtis can probably tell me what I want to know," answered Goff. "Had your father been in good health lately?"

"Much as usual," said Delia. Then she burst into tears.

"Oh, it is horrible!" she sobbed. "It must be my fault. But I didn't know—I never thought..."

"It isn't your fault, darling. He wasn't himself. You couldn't have done anything."

As Margot said this she put her arm round her friend's waist and tried to comfort her. Then she turned to Goff.

"Delia thinks because she went out a little her father was lonely, and that made him do it. Can't you tell her she is wrong? No girl can spend her whole life indoors, can she? It is not as though he was ill—physically ill, I mean."

She looked at Roger and Goff as though demanding that they should help her in her task of compassion.

"It may be as you say," replied the detective. "If she can answer a few questions I shall know better."

He paused a moment. Then as Delia seemed to be getting a little more composed, he began again.

"At what time did you go out last night?"

"Eight o'clock."

"That is quite right," added Margot. "Rhoda and Jimmie Durrant and I came and fetched her and we all went to the theatre."

"To Labour of Love?" asked Roger.

"No. That is Uncle Victor's play. We were there the night before. Last night we went to the Jollity."

"So you got home a little after eleven?" said Goff to Delia.

"No," Margot began.

"Please let her speak for herself," said Goff a little sharply. "I can give her time."

"After the theatre," Delia murmured in a low tone, "we went to the Golden Fleece for supper, and we stayed there till about three. Then we came home."

"Yourself, Miss Watney, and those two she mentioned?"

"Yes—and my cousin."

"Who is he?"

"Wilfrid Mounsey," put in Margot.

"Then you discovered what had happened? I do not want to distress you, but please describe it as well as you can."

"They—they brought me home," said Delia shakily, "and I—I asked them in. They were only here a few minutes and—and when they went I noticed a light under the door of my father's room. I looked in and I—I saw him. . ."

She broke down again.

"Why did I go?" she moaned between her sobs. "Why did I go?"

"When she saw him," went on Margot, "she ran to the door and called us back. We were just starting. She said her father was dead, and then she fainted. We all went in and we telephoned the police."

"The nephew, Wilfrid Mounsey, does not live here?" Roger asked.

"He lives in rooms off the Cromwell Road."

"What is the exact address?" asked Goff.

"Queens Terrace," said Margot.

A note was made of it, and with a glance at the inspector as though asking for permission, Roger enquired: "Did you notice that the wristwatch Mr. Curtis was wearing was broken?"

"Of course I did not," Margot replied a little indignantly. "Nor did Delia. Do you imagine we should think of anything like that?"

"I dare say you would not, but you may be able to tell me this. Mr. Curtis would not have gone on wearing a watch with a broken glass, would he?"

"Who would?" she retorted.

Roger turned to Delia, who was again more controlled. "You, of course, knew your father's wrist-watch? Was it in good order?"

"It was in perfect order and he always said it kept good time."

"One thing I can tell you," said Margot suddenly, "since you want to fuss about everything. When we came in the wireless was on."

"After 1 a.m.?" asked Roger.

"I didn't say it was playing. I said it was on. The direction disc was lit up. I switched it off."

"Why did you do that?"

"I don't know. While we were waiting it caught my eye, and it seemed the sensible thing to do."

Roger made no comment and Goff resumed.

"You did not find, then or since, any letter of explanation or farewell?"

"No—nothing," replied Delia shakily.

"What servants have you?"

"A married couple named Russell."

"Where were they last night?"

"It was their night out."

"What time are they due in?"

"No time, really. I mean they are married and want to go to the theatre like other people."

"They came downstairs while we were waiting," supplemented Margot. "They told me they got in about twelve. They saw nothing and heard nothing."

Goff ignored her, though what she said was no doubt true. "Do they generally come in at the front of the house or through the gardens?"

"At the front. There is a door to the gardens, but servants and tradespeople do not use it."

"Had they used it they would have seen the light in your father's room and would have gone to him?"

"I do not think they would have gone to him," said Delia. "They were off duty till the morning."

"You have to be considerate in these days," Margot added, "even if it is damned uncomfortable."

"Can you account for it," Goff still addressed the daughter of the house, "that no one heard the shot? No one in the street or in the gardens, or in the next-door house?"

"I cannot."

"I think that is a silly question," said Margot. "How do you know no one heard it? What happens if you do hear a shot? You say to yourself, 'What is that?' If there are more shots you may get excited; if there are not, you think it was a back-fire or a door slammed."

Goff looked at her with some disfavour, but Roger guessed she was trying to do her best to make things easier for Delia.

"You went out at eight. Did you suppose that your father would be at home alone, or was he expecting visitors?"

"I thought he would be alone, except—"

Then she again burst into tears.

"Can't you see you are torturing her?" cried Margot furiously. "She is blaming herself that she left him. What the hell is the use of rubbing it in?"

"If you speak to me like that," said Goff, "I shall order you to leave the room."

"And if I refuse to go?" she returned defiantly.

"I shall put you out."

Their eyes met. Goff could be grim enough when he chose. Her eyes dropped.

"I am sorry," she muttered. "I guess I'm a bit on edge, but I only wanted to help."

"Now, Miss Curtis," Goff went on patiently, "you were saying your father was likely to be alone except—except what?"

"Except that I thought my cousin might come in."

"Wilfrid Mounsey?"

"Yes."

"Did he come?"

"Yes."

"At what time?"

"I don't know exactly, but he had said he would come in, and Margot was to be there. Then Margot telephoned that her uncle had given her the tickets for the Jollity and she had fixed up a party afterwards with the Durrants. I was to leave a message for Wilfrid to come on to us at the Golden Fleece, after the show. My father didn't want me to go. He asked me to stay with him. If I had ... if I had ... it ... wouldn't have happened."

Once again she was overcome with sobs. What she said was no doubt in one way true, and her unhappiness was very understandable. Had she stayed with her father, he would not have shot himself. But it would be an entirely unwholesome and unreasonable situation for a girl to have to give up all her normal pleasures under a threat of suicide. It might be that her indifference to her father's wishes, not that night but for many nights, had lessened his desire to live; yet if his mind was so unhinged that self-destruction was possible, the girl might be blaming herself unduly. It would only have been a question of time.

"He had never threatened to harm himself?" Roger asked gently.

"No, n-n-never," was the quavering reply.

"If you want to know about Wilfrid," burst in Margot, "I can tell you. Seeing that he and I are practically engaged to be married, in that at least I know more than Delia."

"What can you tell me?" asked Goff.

"He had a class from eight till nine. He got here about half-past nine, and Mr. Curtis gave him our message. He came along and joined us at supper. He was waiting at the theatre when we got out."

"He had a class?" repeated the detective.

"He is in his uncle's office and is going up for the final in accountancy."

"Thank you," said Goff coldly. "Then, so far as we know at present, Wilfrid Mounsey was the last person to see Mr. Curtis alive, and that would have been about an hour and a half before he shot himself."

He paused a moment, and added as an apparent afterthought: "When you say you are practically engaged—?"

Margot flushed.

"I mean we are really engaged, but I am not allowed to marry before I am twenty-one, and Mr. Curtis would not hear of anything before Wilfrid was through his final."

"Has he been up before?" Roger asked.

"Twice," replied the girl shortly.

A good deal might lie behind that. When a young man fails in his exams his relatives are apt to be critical if he shows undue fondness for the joys of night life. But Wilfrid had evidently attended his class.

"I shall of course be seeing him," said Goff. Then he turned to Delia. "There is nothing more you can tell me?"

"Nothing."

"Your father had not complained of sleeplessness, or anything of that sort? He had not, so far as you are aware, consulted a doctor?"

"I thought he was all right. We never had a doctor."

"Had he any interests outside his home and his business—public affairs, politics and so on?"

"I don't think so," said the girl. "He seldom went out."

"Was he alone in his business?"

"He had Mr. Foyle and some clerks."

"Is Mr. Foyle a partner?"

"He had no partners. Mr. Foyle is his head clerk."

Goff paused a moment. Then he said: "You know, of course, that your uncle, Alexander Curtis, appears to have shot himself at the same time?"

She nodded.

"They were good friends?"

"Yes. Very good friends."

"You cannot suggest any explanation for their both acting in the same way at the same time?"

"N-no," she replied with a sob.

"Anyway," declared Margot stoutly, "it shows Delia has no need to blame herself. There was something we do not know about. There must have been."

Goff made no reply to her comment, for at that moment the constable on duty outside tapped at the door and told them Mr. Marmaduke Curtis had arrived. He wished to see Miss Curtis and also the inspector.

"May we ask him in?" Goff enquired politely of the girl.

"I suppose so," she said.

"Before he comes," Roger remarked, "there is just one thing I would like to know. Was your father keen on the wireless?"

"He generally listened for the news and the more serious talks," she said.

"He hated the music, except the symphony concerts," added Margot, "and Delia loved it. So you can judge."

Apparently she meant that for Delia to have to remain at home with her father when their tastes were so dissimilar was more than it was reasonable to expect.

She however said nothing more and Roger asked no question. The door again opened and Marmaduke Curtis came in.

VI. THE BROTHER

ALEXANDER the home-lover, Frederick the austere and Marmaduke the assertive. That had been Victor Morant's brief summary of the characteristics of the three brothers. Roger Bennion watched with special interest as the sole survivor entered the room.

He was not unlike his brothers, but was rather stouter, his face was fleshier and his eyes were closer together. Roger had only seen the brothers with the pallor of death. Marmaduke had a high colour and gave the impression of one who lived well. He walked across to his niece Delia and kissed her.

"Sorry, my dear, very sorry," he whispered rather huskily. "It is a terrible shock for all of us, but you must be brave."

He shook hands with Margot.

"I know you will try to help her," he said.

Then he turned to the three men, Goff, Roger and Goff's assistant who had silently been taking down everything of importance that was said.

"Which of you is Inspector Goff?"

"I am," Goff replied.

"Mr. Morant telephoned to my office and told me what had happened. He said you were here and that you would wish to see me. So I thought it was best to come along at once. I need hardly say how appalled I am at what has happened. It seems almost too terrible to be true."

"You cannot account for it in any way," Goff asked, "in either case?"

"Indeed I cannot. Of course there were peculiar circumstances, but I should have regarded my brothers as the last men to end their lives in that way."

"What do you mean by peculiar circumstances?"

Marmaduke looked at him and then glanced at the two girls. "That is why I wanted to see you at once," he said, "but what I have to tell you should, I think, be confidential, at any rate for the time being."

"He wants us to go," said Margot to Delia. She was not slow in the uptake, and the two girls moved towards the door. Goff made no motion to restrain them.

"I will see you later, my dear," said Marmaduke to his niece.

The girl gave no reply. She gave the impression that she had no particular affection for her uncle.

"You have, I presume, seen Alexander's widow?" he said as the door closed.

"I have," Goff replied.

"Did you make sure that she was his widow?"

"What do you mean?"

"You did not enquire when and where they were married?"

"Naturally I did not."

"A pity. Helen is ingenious. Her reply might have been interesting."

There was a look of positive malice in his narrow eyes as he said it. Goff's reply was crisp.

"I've no time for riddles. Please tell me plainly what you have to say."

"I will. Alexander and Helen were never married."

"You wish me to believe that a solicitor in his position was living with a woman he had not married."

"It happens to be true," Marmaduke replied, "but it is a very curious story. Of course if Helen can show when and where they were married that is another thing. Though it might be unfortunate for her."

"What is the story?"

"You will understand I am only speaking from a sense of duty."

"Of course," said Goff dryly.

"Ten years ago Alexander told Frederick and myself that he had met a woman he would like to marry. Her name was Helen Robson. But he could not marry her as she had a husband in a lunatic asylum. The husband was incurable, and Alexander spoke very bitterly of the cruelty of the law that tied a young and attractive woman to a hopeless lunatic. He said he meant to regard her before Heaven as his wife, and he asked Frederick and myself to accept her as such."

"You agreed?"

"What could we do? It was his affair, and if we accepted her no one else was likely to question it."

"Did his partner, Mr. Morant, know?" enquired Roger.

"That I cannot tell you. I should doubt it. It was a domestic, not a business matter, and the fewer who heard of it the better. Morant never spoke of it to me, and Frederick and I agreed not to talk about it. Alexander went abroad on holiday and wired that he was married. He brought Helen home and no question was ever raised."

"She is really Mrs. Helen Robson?"

"She changed her name from Robson to Curtis. By deed poll, I believe they call it. That is all the marriage they ever had."

"The husband is still alive?" asked Goff.

"Absolutely potty, but likely to last for years and years. At times I am told he thinks he is a scarecrow. He will tear his clothes to rags and stand on one leg with his arms at odd angles. He can keep it up for hours. That, of course, is harmless enough. But at other times he thinks he is a schoolmaster and everyone he meets wants caning. Then he is really troublesome. I believe he started it on Helen, so she had to get him put away."

There was no doubt Marmaduke relished the story he had to tell, and he watched his listeners to judge its effect.

"Under the new Act," Roger remarked, "a divorce can be obtained in such cases."

Marmaduke leered at him. "That is quite true, and that is where the trouble arose. I asked Alexander what he was going to do about it, and there seemed to be two difficulties. The first was that it is one thing to grant a divorce to a poor suffering wife, the victim of a marriage broken by lunacy, and quite another to give it to a woman who has taken the law into her own hands and lived for years with another man. The court might exercise its discretion in such a case; on the other hand it might not. The other difficulty was rather worse."

"Well?" said Goff.

Marmaduke leered more broadly. "Suppose you lived with a woman and were not happy with her; if the chance came along to make that unhappiness permanent and official, would you jump at it?"

"You say they were not happy?"

"I am sure they were not. Alexander was a quiet, home-loving sort of fellow, but he had a streak of what the writers call romanticism in him. I believe it was pity more than anything else that made him do what he did. He thought he loved her, but I always say choosing a wife is like choosing boots. You ought to be able to try 'em to see if they fit. If they don't, they give you hell. She wasn't a wife, but the same applies. While the old law stood, he would never have let her down. When it was changed and she demanded marriage, he didn't see it that way. Not with her."

It was a curious story. Those who framed the new law giving relief where it was so urgently needed can hardly have foreseen that such circumstances might arise.

"Not with her," Goff repeated. "Do you mean he wanted to marry someone else?"

"I have ideas about that," said Marmaduke, "but I would sooner keep them to myself. You can take it that Alexander was the sort of fireside man who wants a wife, and Helen was not the sort of wife he wanted. It may be he would have liked a family, and that in the circumstances would have been awkward."

It was not a nice smile that Marmaduke gave them. If what he said was true, the tragedy would perhaps have become more understandable—had not both the brothers died.

"Who was the other woman?" Goff asked bluntly.

"That," said Marmaduke, "is a question I must decline to answer."

"So you have nothing more to tell me?"

"On the contrary, there is the most important thing of all. When he took Helen to live with him, Alexander made a will in her favour. This will set out their true relationship and his reasons for what he had done. He called for a change in the law to prevent such things happening again. He thought when he had gone it would be published and would create enough sensation to bring about that change. When the new law was passed his will became silly. So he destroyed it."

"Did he make another?" Roger enquired.

"No."

"You mean a lawyer died without making a will?" demanded Goff.

"Nothing odd in that," shrugged Marmaduke. "Other lawyers have done the same. What do they say about the cobbler's wife being ill-shod? But don't you see the special reason?"

"What special reason?"

"What I have been telling you. Before he made a new will he wanted to come to some arrangement with Helen. He offered her reasonable provision if she would leave him. But she was difficult."

"How do you know this?" Roger asked.

"He told me, a week ago."

"He had the whip-hand," said Goff.

"You might think so," replied Marmaduke, "but it was not so simple as that. Unless he did things her way, Helen threatened to sue her lunatic husband for divorce and to tell the world she had been living with Alexander for ten years. Not a nice prospect for a family solicitor to have it broadcast that he was living in sin!"

Marmaduke gave the impression that the living in sin was a pretty good joke. But he went on: "Naturally Alexander was worried out of his mind. He must either go on living with a woman he had ceased to care for, to marry her perhaps, or the dirty linen would be washed in public."

"You mean," said Goff, "that is the explanation of his suicide?"

"Seems so to me," answered the brother. "He was that sort."

There was a pause. The story became more remarkable, and even if Marmaduke gloated over the telling of it, it was hardly likely he had invented it.

"If what you say is right," Roger remarked, "and he died intestate, his wife, so-called, would get nothing."

"It is right enough," said Marmaduke with obvious satisfaction.

"Who would get what there is?" Goff asked.

"Failing other blood relations," said Roger, "everything would go to his brothers. Or rather, Marmaduke Curtis would get one half and Frederick's daughter, Delia, the other half."

"Is that really the case?" queried Marmaduke.

He tried to sound surprised, but there was little doubt he was well aware of the fact.

"Of course," he went on, "Helen has only herself to blame, but I do not doubt we shall act fairly by her."

Again there was a pause. Goff gave a characteristic grunt.

"You hadn't seen Alexander for a week?"

"That is so," replied the brother, after a moment's hesitation. "He might have made a will during that week without telling you?"

"He might, but in the circumstances it is not likely. I sounded Morant when he rang me up. He knew nothing of such a thing."

"Will or no will," said the detective, "your suggestion is that his suicide is due to worry between the alternatives of living with the woman he disliked and possible scandal if he ceased to do so?"

"Seems that way to me," said Marmaduke. "I cannot think of anything else."

"You realise that I must check up on what you say? I must ask Helen Curtis about it?"

"Of course you must. She ought to have told you."

"Huh. It may all be true, but it does not explain why your other brother Frederick should have shot himself at the same time and in the same way."

"It does not," agreed Marmaduke, "but need there be any connection between the two affairs? Very odd that they should happen together, but things are like that sometimes. Perhaps there is a queer streak in the family. I hope it has missed me."

"You have no theory as to Frederick's suicide?"

"I was not as friendly with Frederick as with Alexander. I don't mean we quarrelled, but we saw less of one another. Frederick's wife died five years ago, and he has not been the same man since. When you marry, as I said just now, you never know how it will turn out. Alexander was miserable because his woman wanted to live with him; Frederick was miserable because his died. He never got over it, and that girl of his and the nephew gave him a lot of trouble."

"In what way?"

"I'm not blaming Delia. She wants to see a bit of life; that is natural enough. But Wilfrid Mounsey is an idle young fool. I am all for a fellow having a good time, but he must earn it. Work doesn't suit Master Wilfrid. He is in his uncle's office, but from what I hear when he was sent out to do the books for some firm they audited, he would let the other chap get on with the job while he went off and played cricket. He'd cut his classes to run around with Delia and Morant's girl, Margot. He was damned impertinent too. But that's not the point. All I mean is that Frederick had a sort of melancholia and they did not help him."

"You know nothing about Frederick's will?" asked Roger.

"Delia gets everything," shrugged Marmaduke, "sure to. Except the Pratt money."

"What is the Pratt money?" Goff enquired.

"There were three sisters, pretty girls all of 'em. One married Frederick, one married Mounsey, and the third married Pratt. Pratt left her a tidy bit, and when she died she left it to her sisters and their husbands for life, and after that to be divided between the nephews and nieces—that is Wilfrid and Delia, there are no others. That may be why Wilfrid doesn't work. Bound to have money someday."

"Much?" asked Roger.

"Half of about thirty thousand."

"He gets it now, on the death of his uncle?"

"I suppose so."

"When did you last see Frederick?" Goff enquired.

"That also was about a week ago."

At that moment the door opened and Margot came in. She crossed to Goff. "I telephoned Wilfrid and said you would want to see him. He has just come and can spare you half an hour."

"Can he indeed?" returned Goff. "Very good of him. Send him in."

VII. THE NEPHEW

"I SHAN'T want you," said Goff sharply to Margot when she returned with a tall curly-haired fellow of about four and twenty.

"You won't want me either," said Marmaduke. "Come along, Margot. Let us see if we can do anything for Delia."

Margot looked mutinous. She obviously would have liked to stay with the young man to whom she said she was engaged, but Goff remembered her previous interruptions and waited for her to go.

"You are Wilfrid Mounsey, Mr. Frederick Curtis's nephew?" he began, as the door closed.

"That's right. This is a ghastly business, isn't it? I can't understand it at all."

"You were in your uncle's office?"

"I was—or I am, whichever way you ought to put it. If you have been talking to smarmy Marmy about me you probably know the worst."

He was dark, with laughing eyes, but a weak mouth. His voice was not unpleasing, though he was perhaps less assured than he wished to appear. Goff continued in his official tone: "I am told you called here last night. If that is right, please let me know just what happened."

Wilfrid considered for a moment, and then he began. "Of course I'm frightfully sorry about Uncle Fred. I can't think why he did it, but I am sure Delia has no need to blame herself as she is doing. He was as hard as nails, and if he meant to shoot himself nothing she or anyone could have done would have stopped him. He didn't enjoy life, so I suppose he found it wasn't worth going on; but the fact that she had a bit of fun sometimes didn't make it any better or any worse, did it?"

"I am asking what happened last night," said Goff.

"Sorry. I thought you wanted to know why I supposed he had done it, and anyway it wasn't Delia's fault. I got here about half-past nine. I asked where Delia and the others were. He told me they had gone to the Jollity, so I pushed off to meet them."

"How long were you with him?"

"About ten minutes; perhaps a quarter of an hour."

"What did you talk about?"

"I told you. I asked where Delia...

"That did not take ten minutes."

Wilfrid grinned. "Rather not. Uncle Fred, as usual, improved the shining hour. He wanted to know just what we had done at the class, and if I meant to get through the exam this time. I said I hoped I would, but it would be far better if he let me do what I really wanted to do."

"What is that?"

"Well—I can sing and dance a bit. I want to have a shot at the films. I know there are crowds who can't get on, but aren't there crowds of accountants, too, who can't get on? If you are going to be a failure, isn't it as well to fail at something you enjoy? I don't think I should fail, but I hate figures and all the blasted debits and credits and balances forward."

"You told him that?"

"More or less."

"And he said?"

"Same as usual. We'd been through it all before. He said my desire to act was just a crazy notion I should grow out of. He had a fine business to hand on and he wanted me to have it."

"You did not quarrel?"

"Quarrel? No. I was itching to get away. I said I would do my best."

"Did he seem depressed, or in any way different from the usual?"

"Not a bit. He was never very gay, you know. He took things too seriously. If accountancy does that for you—

and I guess it must—what is duller than sticking indoors over other people's balance sheets?—I did not want to grow up like it."

"I see."

Goff paused a moment and Roger put a question.

"How did you get into the house?"

"From the garden. The side door. I always do. I went to Delia's room but there was no one there. So I went to his room."

"You just walked in? Is the garden door always open?"

"We generally use it."

"Isn't that rather dangerous? Thieves might get in."

"If they knew about it, but they don't. Besides, they would be seen in the garden."

"Are there people in the garden at night?" Roger asked.

"When it is fine. And there are lots of windows looking on to them."

"But it was not fine last night?"

"Precious seldom is," said Wilfrid.

Then Goff began again.

"You returned with your cousin and the others at about 3 a.m. Is that right?"

"Quite right."

"What happened?"

"Delia asked us in, but we kept quiet as we did not want to disturb anyone. We were only here for a few minutes. Then, as we were getting the car to go, she called us back and said her father had shot himself. She fainted. We went in and found it was true. So I telephoned to the police."

"Except that your uncle was dead, things were just the same as when you were there before?"

"I think so. He was lying on the floor and the revolver was by him. I am afraid I did not look at much else."

"Huh. You know his brother Alexander shot himself at the same time?"

"Margot told me. I cannot understand it. I liked Uncle Alec."

"When you and your friends found Delia's father," Roger enquired, "did you move anything or take anything away?"

"We certainly did not take anything away—why do you ask? It was all pretty ghastly. Delia had fainted; I half-thought she was dead too."

"Did you move your uncle?"

"I—I suppose I did. I guess we lost our heads a bit. I hoped he wasn't really dead."

"How did you know he was dead?" asked Goff.

"He was stone cold—and the wound with the blood on his face—and the revolver."

"Did you know he had a revolver?"

"No."

"Who," Roger enquired, "first noticed the broken wrist-watch?"

"Was it broken? I didn't see that."

"I suppose you didn't see what condition it was in when you were with him at half-past nine?"

"Curious you should ask that," said Wilfrid, "for as a matter of fact, I did. There is no clock in the room and I wasn't sure of the time. I wanted to get away, but I didn't like to look at my own watch while he was talking, so I tried to peep at his."

"Could you see what it said?"

"I might have done, but he saw what I was after and he said in his rather sarcastic way, 'I mustn't keep you.' Made me feel rather an ass, and I was glad to get out. I suppose that sounds heartless. I am fearfully sorry for what happened afterwards, but that is just how it was."

"Had the watch glass been broken," asked Roger, keeping to the point in hand, "would you have noticed it?"

"I think I should."

"Your uncle said he must not keep you," remarked Goff. "You do not think from that he was expecting someone else?"

"It didn't occur to me that way," said Wilfrid.

"Was the wireless on?" asked Roger.

"No."

"You're sure?"

"Quite sure. Our talk didn't exactly ripple, you know. There were pauses. The wireless would have suggested something for me to say."

"Margot Watney told us the wireless was on when you came in at three o'clock. No transmission of course, but the light burning. Did you notice that?"

"Afraid I didn't. I was only thinking of him and Delia."

"Had he been worried or overworked at his office?" Goff enquired.

Wilfrid shook his head. "I should not say so. He left things pretty much to old Foyle, it seemed to me."

There were a few more questions, but, except for his account of his call at nine Wilfrid's story confirmed that told by Margot and Delia and did not add appreciably to it.

"What now?" asked Roger, when he left them.

"I am not satisfied about things," frowned Goff. "Not one little bit. Coincidences up to a point I can accept. For brothers to shoot themselves at the same time might happen. But for them both to do it without adequate reason and without a word of explanation takes a hell of a lot of believing. There must be something in it we don't know."

"You have heard reasons—of sorts," said Roger.

"Being?"

"That Frederick never recovered from the loss of his wife, and Alexander was unable to get rid of his."

"I think my next job," decided Goff, "is to find out if what Marmaduke told us is true. If that woman and Alexander were not married it might make a lot of difference."

Helen Curtis was surprised to see them back so soon. Mr Morant had left, and with the assistance of a maid she was packing when they arrived.

"I cannot stop here," she said. "I am going to a hotel."

Goff saw that the door to the room was closed. Then he put his question. "When were you and Alexander Curtis married?"

The colour faded from her somewhat blotchy cheeks.

"What do you mean?" she asked.

"Just that. When and where were you married?"

It was some moments before she replied. "I suppose Marmaduke has been talking to you?"

"Does that matter? I am asking for facts."

"You mean you know we were not married?"

"I would like you to tell me about it yourself. It would have been better if you had done so at first."

"What difference does it make? It doesn't alter the fact that Alexander shot himself."

"It may explain the reason," said Goff patiently.

She looked at him with an expression far from pleasant. Then she muttered: "If you tell me what Marmaduke said, I will let you know if it is true."

"He said that your husband, a Mr. Robson, is alive and is in an asylum. Is that right?"

"It is right," she replied defiantly.

"He also said there had been some difference between you and his brother as to what you should do as a result of the new Act that would allow you to divorce Mr. Robson."

"Well?"

"Is that true?"

There was a longer pause. When she replied her voice was bitter. "Marmaduke always hated me. He made mischief whenever he could. When he spoke to me there was always that devilish grin of his as though he wanted me to know he could give me away if he chose. Now he has done it."

"I am not discussing Marmaduke," said Goff. "I have to find out why Alexander shot himself, and I want to know how things were between you and him."

"Is it wrong of me to want to marry when the law says I can?" she demanded more passionately. "Alexander had the best years of my life. Was it likely I would give him up to some other woman? Hadn't I suffered enough? Eight years of hell with Radnor Robson before they put him away, then ten years of Marmaduke's mockery. Was I not entitled to a square deal at the finish, or is that only for men?"

"Alexander Curtis did not wish to marry you?" commented Goff quietly.

"He said it might cause scandal!" she cried a little wildly. "I promised him all the scandal he wanted if he didn't!"

"So things were strained between you? That may be why he shot himself."

"If it is, it won't do him or anyone else any good to make it public, will it?"

"That may be unavoidable," said Goff. "Do you know anything of the provisions of his will?"

"Not yet. I asked Mr. Morant, but he doesn't know either. There was a will; I suppose that stands."

"Unless he destroyed it."

"Unless he destroyed it," she repeated. "Why do you say that?" There was fear in her eyes and her face was paler than before.

"Marmaduke said so."

"Marmaduke—that devil! Where shall I be if there is no will?"

"That is for the lawyers to ascertain," Goff murmured.

"Oh, the cheats! The devils!" Tears began to flow and she became almost hysterical. "Yes! We quarrelled! He wanted to get rid of me after all I had been to him! He offered me something, but it was not enough. And I wanted to be straight. Was that wrong? Marmaduke was behind it all. I am sure he was. He always hated me."

She sobbed for some moments, hard, angry sobs. It did not seem she was sorry for the man she had lost, only for herself.

"You say there was another woman?" said Goff quietly. "Will you tell me her name?"

"I don't know why I shouldn't. Dreda Costello. Calls herself an artist. Pretends she would enjoy the stodgy life he wanted to lead."

"Where does she live?"

"In Chelsea. Beaufoy Studios."

"Did he wish to marry her?"

"He did. I was to be thrown on the scrap-heap! But if he made no will she gets nothing either. Thank Heaven for that! Who does get it?"

"That is not my affair," said Goff, "and the facts have to be verified. If they are as stated, his brothers or their heirs might get it."

"That means Marmaduke! The devil looks after his own!"

Other calls had to be paid. Goff liked to cover as much of the ground himself as he could. A brief visit to Colston Court, South Kensington, seemed happily timed. Mrs. Parr was just going out when the inspector with Roger arrived.

"You are related to Mrs. Helen Curtis of Hans Avenue?" he began, after he had explained who he was.

"She is my sister."

Evelyn Parr had never been beautiful. She was apparently older than Helen, but had grown thinner, not stouter, with the years. Her flat was small and rather shabby, but she herself was smartly dressed with the latest oddity in hats on her head. She seemed a blunt, matter-of-fact sort of woman.

"When did you last see her?"

"Last night. We went to the theatre together."

"What theatre?"

"The Cardinal. She had some tickets, so we dined at the Troc and then saw the show. Why are you asking me these questions? Helen telephoned me that Alexander had shot himself, but I do not see that I can help you."

"It is a matter of routine," explained Goff; "you will understand that. When did she telephone?"

"This morning. I was just going to her—poor thing. Wasn't it awful for her? I think suicide is so cowardly. It is all right for the one who goes, but he thinks nothing of the shock for those who are left behind."

Goff did not digress into discussion. "You knew her husband?" he asked.

"Of course I did, but I have not seen him for more than a year."

"You were not friendly?"

"He was—well, he is dead, so I won't say it. We had no use for one another."

"Was the marriage a perfectly normal one?"

"Just what do you mean?" asked Mrs. Parr.

"Were you present at the wedding?"

"I was not."

"Where did it take place?"

The sister looked hard at him for some moments. Then she said: "Either you have put these questions to Helen, or you haven't. Which is it?"

"I have," replied Goff calmly.

"Then she has told you. Why ask me?"

"It is my job to confirm what I am told. Please tell me what you know about it."

"Helen has been unlucky. She married Radnor Robson when she was young. He was a brute and is now in a lunatic asylum. She and Alexander have been married in name for ten years."

"They were not happy together?"

"She would have been a good wife if he would have let her."

"But they were talking of separating?"

"Were they? All I know is that Helen wanted to marry him now that it is legal to do it."

"But he refused?"

"That shows the sort of man he was. Not normal. That is why he shot himself."

VIII. THE MANAGING CLERK

Later that day a visit was paid to the London Wall offices of Frederick Curtis the accountant. Inspector Goff and Roger Bennion were received by a man who introduced himself as Charles Foyle, and said he was Mr. Curtis's managing clerk.

"How long have you been with him?" asked the detective, a little surprised perhaps that the holder of so important a position was not of a more venerable appearance, especially as Wilfrid Mounsey had called him old Foyle.

"I might almost say all my life," said Foyle. "I came here when I was fourteen. Later on Mr. Curtis gave me my articles, and last year, when Mr. Singleton retired, he made me manager. I have been here twenty-four years. I owe everything to him and I am inexpressibly shocked by what has happened."

"Can you explain it?" asked Goff crisply.

"Indeed I cannot. When I had the message I could not at first believe it."

"The business is flourishing?"

"Never more so. Only yesterday we got an important new account, the Woodfall Packing Company Limited. There are several matters on which I need direction at this present moment. It is very distressing. The whole staff feels it just as I do. He was very good to all of us."

"His health and his manner latterly had been normal?"

"Had you asked me that a day ago," Foyle replied, "I should have said yes, without hesitation. In view of what has happened, one naturally tries to account for things."

"What do you mean?"

Foyle seemed to find it a little difficult to express himself. He was very neatly attired and Roger, considering him carefully, guessed that his first action on hearing the bad news had been to send out for the black tie he was now wearing.

Of middle height, thin, and with the sallow complexion of an indoor worker, his eyes were quick and intelligent. There was something a little obsequious in his manner. It may be that a professional man who has not had a public school training seldom acquires the easy assurance of one who has. No doubt he was a wizard with books, and that is what his employer would have required.

"Mr. Curtis," he was saying, "was a deeply religious man. That, of course, is hardly consistent with suicide. On the other hand he used to study the prophecies in the Bible and he tried to fit them to present world conditions. He would sometimes say the end was near. I remember once he told me that it was prophesied that the stars would fall and that everyone from kings and chief captains to common men and slaves would hide in dens and in holes in the mountains. He said that clearly foretold modern air warfare. He talked sometimes of the Anti-Christ."

"Hitler?" asked Roger.

"No, sir. Stalin, or Stalin's successor. Hitler, he said, would collapse and a demoralised Germany would be swallowed up by Russia, and then would come the Armageddon. I am afraid it did not mean a lot to me."

"Are you suggesting that these ideas turned his brain?" Goff enquired.

"I don't like to say that because up to yesterday he seemed in every other way so shrewd and practical. He did say, when the day came, those who lived to see it would wish they were dead. But it seemed remote; I never took it seriously."

"Had his brother Alexander similar ideas?" asked Roger.

"I did not know Mr. Alexander very well, sir; only, I mean, in business; but Mr. Frederick told me he and his brother used to discuss these things."

"You heard that Alexander Curtis also shot himself?" put in Goff.

"I did. It is terrible. I regarded them both as such—I hardly know how to put it—as such wise, well-balanced men."

"The nephew, Wilfrid Mounsey, works here, doesn't he?"

"He does."

"Was his uncle worried about him?"

Again Foyle hesitated and seemed to choose his words with care. "Mr. Wilfrid is a very pleasant young gentleman. When he settles down he should do quite well. His uncle was disappointed that he did not do better in his exams."

"They were on good terms?" enquired Goff.

"Except for that, they were. Everyone likes Mr. Wilfrid, but his heart is not in his work. This trouble may make all the difference. Mr. Curtis used to say—but perhaps I had better not go into that."

"No harm in telling me," said Goff.

"Mr. Curtis used to say that Mr. Wilfrid had plenty of ability and that perhaps—some day—when he was qualified, he and I might carry on together. That is, of course, when Mr. Curtis retired."

"You were to be a partner?" Roger asked.

"Yes, sir; in a small way. I do not mean he promised it to me, but all the clients know me, and Mr. Wilfrid would want someone of experience with him."

"Was Mr. Curtis talking of retiring?"

"Only vaguely, sir, as men do. Perhaps it was meant more as an inducement to Mr. Wilfrid than a promise to me. I never thought of him retiring for a good many years yet."

"But when he did, you and Mr. Wilfrid would carry on?"

"That was the idea," Foyle replied. "Some while back I had rather a good offer elsewhere. When I told him of it, that was what he said. It really all waited for Mr. Wilfrid."

Foyle was naturally ambitious. From office boy or very junior clerk he had become manager. No doubt he looked forward to the day when his faithful service would be rewarded with a partnership. How the sudden death of his employer would affect him, he could not tell. He was quite frank about it.

"It is difficult to know what to do in a one-man business; there is no one to give instructions. We have a number of very important matters in hand. Had anything happened to Mr. Frederick in the ordinary way I should have gone to Mr. Alexander. But for them both to die the same night—it is such a shock. I feel so utterly bewildered. I want to do my best for Miss Delia, but who is to give me instructions?"

"What about the other brother, Mr. Marmaduke?" enquired Roger. "Or Mr. Morant?"

"I don't think Mr. Morant knew his private affairs. Mr. Marmaduke might, but—"

"But what?" snapped Goff.

"Well—Mr. Marmaduke and Mr. Frederick were not such good friends as Mr. Frederick and Mr. Alexander."

"You will soon know something," said Roger. "When the will is found there are pretty sure to be instructions for the carrying on of the business. You will hear from the executors. In the mean time you have a very good excuse for keeping things waiting."

"That is true," Foyle said. "I owe so much to Mr. Frederick that I want to do all I possibly can in his interests. No doubt Mr. Wilfrid will help me."

IX. ROGER SUMS UP

"WE have been busy collecting facts," said Goff, "now we must see what we make of them."

He and Sergeant Queen and Roger Bennion were finishing an evening meal in a quiet corner of a restaurant near Charing Cross. The theatre crowd had gone and it was too early for supper. Goff knew the place well and was aware that he was reasonably safe from interruption.

"A day in the life of a policeman," murmured Roger. "A bit hectic for my taste in an ordinary way."

Goff and his assistants had all been busy. The attendants at the service flats where Alexander Curtis lived had been interviewed. So had the Russells, the married couple who "did for" Frederick Curtis. Calls had been made on neighbours. There had been another talk with Victor Morant at the office of Morant and Curtis. A visit to the studio of Miss Dreda Costello established the fact that she was in the Isle of Wight. Examination had been made of the papers and effects of the dead men. All the usual steps had been taken, but no further explanation had been found that could in any way account for the simultaneous suicide of the two brothers. Enquiries were still proceeding in many directions. Goff was anxious to know when they had obtained the pistols they had used and what communications, if any, had passed between them on the fatal night.

"It may have been hectic for me," said Goff in reply to Roger's comment, as he filled the pipe he had forgotten the night before, "but I have never known you so quiet."

"I have been watching the crime machine in action," replied Roger. "If like the sailor's parrot I have said little, I have thought a devil of a lot."

"Well, spill it."

"Like you, I accept coincidence up to a point, but beyond that point I get sceptical."

"Huh," grunted Goff.

"In the first place I think you have to consider whether you are dealing with two cases of suicide, or one case of suicide and one of murder, or two cases of murder."

Goff looked hard at him and pulled on his pipe.

"You think there is evidence of murder?"

"I am quite sure you do," replied Roger.

"But that lands us in a worse coincidence than ever. Two murders in the same way and at the same time! I dare say you noticed I made enquiries as to their political activities and that sort of thing. In these days of secret societies, people do get liquidated, as they call it, or they may get in a jam and eliminate themselves. Such things are very rare in this country, but so far as we can ascertain neither Alexander nor Frederick was mixed up in anything of the sort. Very much the reverse. They were ordinary professional men whose habits were, if anything, unusually quiet and retiring."

It was a long speech for Goff and showed the matter was worrying him quite a lot.

"Suppose for the moment," said Roger, "we forget about the coincidences and regard the cases separately, each on its merits."

"Go ahead."

"In Alexander's case we have a very curious story. He met a young woman with a husband in a lunatic asylum and, perhaps from quixotic motives, perhaps from ordinary impulses of affection, he passed her off to the world as his wife. As happens in a certain percentage of unions, regular or otherwise, this was not a success. In spite of that, when circumstances changed and it became possible for him to marry, the woman was anxious for him to do so."

"What did you think of her?" put in Goff.

"I thought she was a strong argument for the permanence of marriage—from the woman's point of view. Would any man, having the chance of getting rid of her, wish to bind the shackles tighter? I admit she has had a raw deal, but was not his worse? He took her when she was in trouble; he gave her a home, and made her his wife as far as it was possible to do so. How did she repay him? She was hard and selfish and was no real companion for him. But it is not a question which of them was the more to blame. The thing is, they decided to separate; it was only a question of terms. And at that moment, when he had hopes of getting his liberty, and when he had found another woman he thinks will make him happy, he commits suicide. Is that logical?"

"I have yet to know what the Costello young woman says about it," replied Goff. "Suppose she had turned him down?"

"Morant gave another explanation," remarked Sergeant Queen. "Depression from war scare."

"But Morant did not regard the explanation as adequate," Roger retorted. "I admit Miss Costello's story will be important, though Helen Curtis seemed to have no doubt of her willingness to do as Alexander desired. But let us leave theories and get to facts. How came that clock on the floor?"

"When he fell," said Queen, "he knocked it over."

"Reconstruct the crime," Roger suggested. "This table is about as broad as his desk. Helen Curtis told us his clock always stood at the back near the left-hand corner. She pretended not to be so sure when I pressed her on the point, but the maid who cleans the room was emphatic about it; the clock was always there. Of course it was. Anyone having a clock on a desk puts it at the back, out of the way of his papers. So this mustard pot is the clock."

Roger took the article in question and placed it in the far corner. "Now, Queen, you stand up and shoot yourself so that you fall away from the table, where the body was found, and yet knock the clock over so that it lies level with your shoulder."

"It is not possible," said Goff.

"It is not possible if the clock was where you say," agreed the sergeant, "but suppose for once in a way it was not? Suppose for some reason he had put in at the front?"

"Even then he would not have upset it if he fell away from the table."

"He might have dropped it and not troubled to pick it up."

"Or he could have held it in one hand while he shot himself with the other," said Roger, "but is it likely?"

"I am not saying it is likely, sir," persisted Queen stoutly, "but I do say it's a tall order to ask a coroner's jury to find a verdict of murder just because a clock is on the floor."

"There I agree with you," Roger said. "You have to know a lot more before you can ask a jury for any sort of verdict. It is not the fact that the clock was on the floor that matters, but what the clock was meant to tell us. It stopped at two minutes to eleven. Therefore the man shot himself at two minutes to eleven. Therefore, if there is any suspicion of foul play, the person with an alibi at two minutes to eleven must be innocent."

"The doctor said the time of death was right," Queen observed.

"The doctor was called some time after seven the next morning. He would know the man had been dead from seven to ten hours. No doctor would really be much more precise. But when there is the clock to give the time that seems good enough."

"You believe the woman did it!" exclaimed the sergeant. "I dare bet you are right. Don't you agree, sir?"

He put the question to Goff, who had been saying very little. He had talked a lot during the day, now he was more interested in listening.

"She got in about twelve," Queen went on, thrilled with his new idea. "They had another quarrel and she shot him. Then she altered the clock to two minutes to eleven, stopped it, and put it by his side. She went to her room and had only to wait for someone to find the body and fix the suicide for a time when she could prove she was just leaving the theatre. It fits."

"Is that what you mean, Mr. Bennion?" asked Goff.

"More or less, it is. A man with friends and relations, and according to accounts with a woman he loves, does not as a rule destroy himself without leaving some sort of a message. Pens and paper were at hand, but the only sign is the upset clock. I say it all points to murder, and the time on the clock means nothing. But I am not prepared without a lot more evidence to say that Helen Curtis was the murderer."

"By his death she loses everything," said Goff.

"But she did not know it!" Queen put in quickly. "She gave herself away. She was unaware that the will was destroyed. She said so."

"That is quite true," Roger agreed. "Apparently she was trying to drive a hard bargain with him. Knowing the terms of the old will, and believing it still stood, she might have thought his death would give her more than she would otherwise get. But, as things are, Marmaduke benefits and she does not."

"You mean that Marmaduke—" began Queen.

"All I mean," Roger said, "is that I believe murder was done. Whether Helen, or Marmaduke, or someone else did it, is for you to find out. Of course when you get into touch with Dreda Costello you may learn something. If, for instance, she had a letter of farewell it will prove my ideas are wrong."

"I have been thinking myself much of what you have been saying," Goff commented slowly, puffing at his pipe.

"But what about the other affair? You have still the queer coincidence of the time. Two minutes to eleven in each case."

"That is not the coincidence," replied Roger. "Everyone knows the theatres empty about eleven, so that is a good time to fix for the crime if you have been, or are going to be, at a theatre. The coincidence is that two brothers should be killed in the same way and on the same night."

"That was murder too?" Goff asked

"Do you doubt it? Frederick Curtis loathed popular music. I have looked at yesterday's programme. His wireless was tuned in to National. From 9.30 to 10 the B.B.C. dance band was performing, and from 10 to 11 the Hot-Timers from the Hotel Superb were in full blast. Someone switched it on, but it was not Frederick Curtis. Why they did it, I do not know. Possibly because it made a noise, possibly because it was desired to give the impression that he was alive and listening. It was an error of judgment."

"But a jury will not say it was murder because the wireless was on!" protested Queen.

"Nor would I," said Roger. "Some programmes, horrible music or morbid poetry, might drive people to murder or suicide, but that is a minor point. How did his watch-glass get broken?"

"When he fell," said the sergeant.

"But on what did he hit it? The only hard object within reach was the mahogany desk. Perhaps you noticed it? A beautiful piece of wood, with a perfect polish. Not a scratch anywhere. I looked carefully to see. Can you break a watch-glass on polished mahogany and not leave a mark? The chair was of padded leather and the carpet a thick Turkey. On the carpet, beside the watch, as perhaps you noticed, were some fine splinters of glass."

"Then how did it break?" asked the sergeant.

"My suggestion," Roger replied, "is that when the hands were set to the time selected—and perhaps eleven was chosen for the reason I mentioned—the watch was hit with some hard article, possibly the butt of the revolver, and that smashed the glass and stopped the works. So another alibi was established!"

"Why did you not say this while we were there?" Goff wanted to know.

"I thought you probably saw all I saw, but in any case it was desirable to hear all we could before we hinted at suspicions."

"I am glad you were there," said the inspector frankly. "I had my doubts in the first case but not in the second. Who would have shot Frederick Curtis?"

"Our police," replied Roger, "are wonderful. I am sure a little thing like that will not baffle them for long!"

When he reached his home he was rung up by his crime-news friend, Gordon Lisle.

"Just heard about those Curtis suicides. I am told you were with Inspector Goff all day enquiring into them. Anything for me?"

"Possibly quite a lot," said Roger. "But you must get it from Goff. He left his pipe here last night, so when I took it back I was rewarded with a peep behind the scenes. But I could not say how far what I saw is fit for publication, and I know how particular you are!"

X. MARGOT IN DISTRESS

ROGER BENNION supposed that his active concern in the tragedies of the Curtis brothers was ended. His day in the life of a policeman had been interesting, and he hoped his suggestions had been helpful. How far they already occurred to Inspector Goff he could not tell; but he realised the eminent detective would deal with the affair in his usual efficient way and would not want to take an amateur with him when he pursued his steady but relentless enquiries.

Nor was Roger without occupation of his own. Naturally he felt a very keen interest in the further unravelling of the case, but he and his father had been offered an estate in the Highlands that might afford an opportunity for profitable development, and he had gone north to see what could be done with it.

He was away for the best part of a week, and although he often thought of the coincidences of the double suicide—or murder—he was out of reach of London papers and was unaware of what was actually happening.

When he got back, late on a Friday afternoon, his man Froy told him that a young woman had been ringing him up and seemed very anxious to speak to him.

"Name of Watney, sir. Been through six times at least."

Watney—that must be Margot, niece to Victor Morant and engaged unofficially to Wilfrid Mounsey, nephew of Frederick Curtis.

Roger rang the number she had given and Margot herself answered the call.

"Yes, I do want to see you," she said, in reply to his enquiry. "May I come round?"

"I will come to you, if you like."

"Can you come now?" She indeed sounded anxious.

"I will."

Mr. Morant and his niece had a spacious and attractive flat in a comparatively quiet position behind Victoria Street. The hum of distant traffic could always be heard though little actually passed the building.

The door of the flat was opened by Margot.

"I was watching for you," she said. "I saw you get out of the taxi."

"I have been in Sutherland," he remarked. "Only just back."

"Your man told me. This is my room."

The whole suite appeared sumptuously appointed, with costly rugs and genuine old furniture. The little room into which she led him, her own "den," was as comfortable as a man's room, with its soft low chairs and its luxurious divan; but the colour scheme of green and fawn was essentially feminine. Roger was glad to miss the bizarre note of brilliant clashing hues favoured by some young people.

"Did you accuse Wilfrid of murdering his uncle?" she demanded abruptly, almost before he had time to seat himself.

"Certainly I did not."

"He has been arrested."

She flung the words at him. There was no doubt as to her strained and nervous condition, but her manner astonished him. Why had she sent for him to tell him something he was bound to hear within a few hours?

"I got no news while I was away," he said. "The local journal was only interested in local affairs."

"But it was you who told them it was murder. It must have been. You asked the questions about the watch-glass and the wireless."

"Please do not imagine Inspector Goff overlooked such things. Still less that he would act on vague suggestions from me."

"Uncle Victor told me that you had been concerned in other cases. That you had sometimes been right when the police were wrong. They are wrong now, devilishly wrong. Will you be on their side or ours?"

The girl looked at him with tragedy in her eyes. When Goff had questioned her she had answered him with spirited defiance. Her manner now was very different. The arrest of the man she loved had indeed changed her. But Goff did not make arrests without good reason.

"I suppose Wilfrid has a good lawyer? Is your uncle acting for him?"

"Yes. And he has the best possible counsel. But we want some thing more. We want something more."

She clenched her little hands in her distress. Roger felt uncomfortable.

"I am sure everything that should be done will be done," he said.

"But you know what lawyers are! They squabble over words, and if things look bad anything may happen. We must find out who really did it."

"The law does not often make mistakes."

"How can you tell that?" she cried passionately. "How can anyone tell? Who knows how many innocent people may have suffered while we comfort ourselves by saying the law does not make mistakes?"

He did not reply. After a moment she went on in a lower tone: "I am sorry. You mean there is no reason why you should trouble about it, even if it was your questions that led to his arrest."

"That is not quite fair."

"I think it is. When Uncle Victor told me how wonderful you had been I thought you might help me. But since you say the law is always right—I am sorry."

She broke off abruptly and got up for him to go. But he did not go. It was not the flattery that detained him but the look of despair in her eyes.

"I said the law seldom makes mistakes. The police often do. That is a very different thing."

"You will help us?" Hope shone in her eyes.

"At the present moment all I know is that Wilfrid has been arrested. If you told me all about it, I could give you my opinion—for what it is worth."

For some silent moments their eyes met. It might well be that she was weighing a grave decision.

"If you knew the facts, and they justified it, you would help us to find the real murderer?"

"I would," Roger said, "as far as I could."

There was another silence. Then she began: "I told you Wilfrid and I were to marry."

"You did."

"Wilfrid and I must marry."

Again their eyes met. Then she looked away. Did she mean what the words implied?

"You must marry?"

"Yes. Soon."

She spoke in a very low tone, but there was no doubt of her meaning. He showed that he understood, but he made no reply.

"You think I have been wicked?"

Still he did not speak. He realised the tragic horror of her position and it was not for him to condemn. But what was he to say? How did her unhappy plight affect Wilfrid Mounsey's innocence or guilt?

"Was I wicked?" she went on more passionately, in answer to her own question. "Or was it wicked to make such a will? Have girls no flesh and blood before they are twenty-one? What of the hundreds who marry before they are even twenty?"

"Tell me about the will," Roger said gently. If that was the key to the trouble he must understand it. And it would be easier to talk first of something less intensely personal.

"My father's will. Both my parents died when I was little. I was not to marry without Uncle Victor's consent before I was twenty-one."

"He refused his consent?"

"Frederick Curtis said Wilfrid must not marry until he was through with his exams. Uncle Victor thought he was right."

"What was to happen if you married without consent?"

"I am not quite sure. I lose a good deal. Of course I don't get anything till I am twenty-one."

"And Wilfrid has nothing?"

"Not yet."

"Your uncle and Mr. Curtis were not altogether unreasonable, were they?" Roger asked mildly. "When you anticipated things, did you not realise that this might happen?"

"I thought I was wise to it all," she said. "Anyway I did not suppose Uncle Victor would refuse if it became necessary. Perhaps you have never been in love?"

"I have heard a lot about it," he returned dryly. "Does anyone else know what you have told me?"

"No. But you see what it means? Wilfrid is innocent. I know he is. But you do see that I must prove it?"

"I do see that you are in a very difficult position," he said. A banal remark perhaps, but his sympathy was genuinely aroused. Whether what he had heard was to the young man's credit might be doubted, though possibly Margot's was the stronger nature and hers was at least part of the blame. But for an unmarried girl to find herself with child by a man who was arraigned for murder was as terrible a thing as he could imagine. Terrible for the girl; terrible for the child. No doubt there were excuses for the wrong-doing. Roger regarded himself as old-fashioned in such matters, though no one could be blind to the change in moral values in modern thought and literature. But this presented a problem beyond ordinary experience. If he could help, he felt he must do it. Margot had judged him rightly in that.

"Tell me just what has happened," he said. "So far as you know, why was he arrested?"

"He went back to the house a second time."

"He told us he called to see you and Delia, and his uncle informed him you had gone to the theatre. He said he followed you there; but actually he came back to the house again?"

"That is right," nodded Margot.

"Why did he do that?"

"He had bought me some chocolates. He put them down when he went in to see Mr. Curtis and then forgot them. So he went back for them."

"Why did he not say so before?"

"He didn't see his uncle the second time," Margot explained "so he did not think it mattered."

"Of course you got your chocolates?"

"No. He must have left them in the taxi. He does forget things. We made enquiries and found the taxi-man, but he swears he never had them."

"He may be lying, or his next fare may have taken them. How did this come out?"

"The police called on the other people in the square and a Colonel Parsons who lives on the opposite side of the gardens told them he saw someone go into Mr. Curtis's house and come out again. Then he saw him go back. A little later he heard what might have been a shot and he saw someone come out. You see what a ghastly muddle it is? He must have seen Wilfrid go in the second time, but he was only there a few moments. He went and someone else came, but Colonel Parsons must have missed that. Then he saw that someone go and he thought it was Wilfrid."

Margot looked at him pleadingly, as though begging him to believe it was as she said.

"It could have been that way," Roger commented. "How positive was Colonel Parsons in his identification?"

"I don't know," said the girl unhappily. "I have not seen him. It was what Uncle Victor learnt from the police. But two people might look alike in the dark, across the garden, mightn't they? I mean anyone would suppose the person who went out must be the same as the one they saw go in?"

"If Colonel Parsons heard a shot, why did he do nothing about it?"

"He was not sure it was a shot, and then he heard the wireless. He didn't think about it again till the police asked him."

"It is a pity," said Roger, "that Wilfrid did not tell of his return call in the first place. Things always look so much worse when the police are left to discover them."

"There is something else."

"What is that?"

"The police say Wilfrid's finger-prints are on the revolver."

Roger stared at her. She might well be frightened at the future. She was calmer and more controlled, but he could see what an effort it was. He waited a moment before he replied, and then endeavoured to speak as though the point was not so overwhelming.

"How does Wilfrid account for that?"

"He cannot. But I can. He could, if he were not so honest."

"How do you account for it?"

"Oh, I know how damning it is!" she cried. "You need not pretend. They say no finger-prints are alike and that the hand that touched the revolver must have fired it. But it isn't true. Wilfrid did not do it. He couldn't. When Delia called us in we were all so scared we did not know what to do. We did not know what we did do. Wilfrid tried to help his uncle and he must have picked up the revolver. He doesn't remember that he did. We don't remember seeing him do it. But it must have been that way. Isn't it a thing anyone might do?"

"They might," agreed Roger a little doubtfully. "It would be very unfortunate."

"But we weren't policemen, wise to the tricks and the risks. We lost our heads. Surely it really proves he was innocent?"

"How does it do that?"

"If he had shot him, wouldn't he know his finger-prints might be there? If he hadn't wiped them off, wouldn't he have picked it up and let us all see it in his hand?"

She spoke eagerly; terribly anxious that he should say she was right.

"Something might be made of such a point," said Roger, "but the position is certainly difficult. He never mentioned his second visit until someone else told of it. He accounted for it by saying he went back for chocolates, but the chocolates never appeared. And his finger-prints are on the weapon that was used."

"You believe he did it?"

"I am considering the case as Inspector Goff sees it. There is also a motive, isn't there? I mean from the police point of view? On his uncle's death Wilfrid gets a good deal of money—is that right?"

"It is right enough, but Wilfrid is not that sort."

"I hope not. You are sure he does not know the truth about you?"

"No one knows," she flushed. "I told you because he needs your help. I cannot possibly tell him now; it would make him more utterly miserable."

She herself was near breaking point, but the affair had to be considered in all its aspects.

"Whether you tell your uncle," said Roger slowly, "is for you to decide, but otherwise the fewer who know it the better."

"I shall not tell anyone if you will help us," she muttered, "but what difference could it make?"

"If it were known, it might be assumed that Wilfrid was aware of it. That would appear to make the motive stronger."

"In what way?"

"He would have the further incentive to get money to enable him to marry without delay."

"He didn't know; he mustn't know," she said in a very subdued tone. "I only just knew myself. I was meaning to tell him and to ask if we should get secretly married, or if it would be better to own up to Uncle Victor when—when this happened."

Roger nodded. To blame would be easy enough, but wrongdoing seems sometimes to escape punishment and sometimes to be punished with excessive ferocity. If Wilfrid was in fact innocent, Margot's position and his were indeed desperate.

"There is one thing about which I am not clear," he said. "If Wilfrid left the house for the second time at about nine-forty, what was he doing until nearly eleven—not driving round in a taxi with a box of chocolates?"

"When Mr. Curtis told him we were at the theatre and might be going on somewhere to supper, he knew we should dance, so he went to his rooms to change. He walked there and took the taxi afterwards to the theatre."

"He didn't by any chance leave the chocolates in his rooms?"

"No. He remembers taking them into the taxi."

"Did he tell you he had had them and forgotten them?"

She hesitated. Perhaps it was a temptation to say she had been told about them. But she stuck to the truth.

"Not until afterwards. He thought we should rag him about it. He got them because he understood we were to be indoors with Delia. There is no point in buying chocolates when you are going to a supper and dance. Is it important?"

"Little things sometimes carry a lot of weight. Those chocolates are his explanation of why he went to the house the second time. If he had given them to you, it would lend colour to the story. But since he did not even mention them, and there is no trace of them, it may be contended they were an invention to explain his return after someone had told of it."

"Can't we do anything?" she whispered tragically.

"Quite a lot," he replied, more cheerily than he really felt. "I will see Inspector Goff, but first I think a call on Colonel Parsons might be useful."

"Could I come with you?" she asked eagerly. "It is so ghastly to be doing nothing."

"I think you might," he began. She interrupted.

"There is Uncle Victor. Will you see him? Of course you won't say—"

"I won't. But I would like to see him."

Margot had heard her uncle enter the flat. She went from the room and returned with him.

"Mr. Bennion has agreed to help us," she said.

"That is splendid," beamed the solicitor. "I said you young people ought to know one another: you seem to have managed it without my help." Then he added more gravely to Roger, "You have heard about Wilfrid Mounsey?"

"Margot has just told me," Roger replied. "I have been away in Scotland and have lost touch with things. Have there been any developments in the other case?"

"Not so far as I am aware. At both the inquests open verdicts were returned. In the matter of my poor partner it is of course still possible that it was suicide. But I gather that is not your view, and I find it hard to believe myself."

"If one was murder," declared Margot, "both were, and probably by the same person or group of people. That proves Wilfrid is innocent, as no one suggests he went near Mr. Alexander Curtis."

"I am afraid, my dear, we cannot argue that because he did not kill Alexander therefore he did not kill Frederick," her uncle said. "But we will do our best. I have briefed Sir Norman French, who is the finest man for the job, and we are making all the enquiries we can. There are many awkward features. Has Mr. Bennion any suggestions?"

He looked towards Roger as he spoke and added: "I have heard of your success in other cases. If there has been a mistake here we are lucky to have you with us."

"It might be useful to offer a reward for the person who took the chocolates."

"I see the idea," said the solicitor. "It would support part at least of Wilfrid's story. But you are asking someone to admit they were guilty of a misdemeanour. If the reward were enough, you might get too many to own to it."

"You never can tell," Margot asserted. "We ought to try everything."

"We will, my dear. Mr. Bennion shall draw up the advertisement. Anything else?"

"It wants a bit of thought," Roger replied. "I cannot say what Goff may be willing to tell me, but I might learn something from this Colonel Parsons."

"We must not tamper with witnesses," Morant remarked, "but it is useful to know just what we are up against. Don't you think we might ask Mr. Bennion to spend the week-end with us at Ashcomb, my dear, if he can spare the time? Then he can tell us what he has done and we can discuss things more leisurely."

"Will you?" said the girl eagerly to Roger.

"It is only a little place in Huntingdon," added her uncle. "Easy to get at. I think we can make you comfortable."

"I would like to come," said Roger.

"Oh, thank you!" cried the girl. "Now we can see Colonel Parsons. I will get my hat."

She ran from the room and the solicitor turned to Roger with something of a sigh.

"You see how it is? She and young Wilfrid Mounsey were getting to like one another quite a lot. I don't think there would really have been anything in it, and I am not sure he is the man I would have chosen for her, but this affair has made her his champion She is so sure he is innocent and is so anxious to fight his battles for him."

Roger thought how often it happened that those who were nearest were the most blind to what went on around them. It was very evident that Mr. Morant had no idea how things stood between the accused man and his niece. Fathers, and it may be uncles, do not realise how quickly the girl-child may become a woman. There is little change in themselves between forty and fifty, and they sometimes seem to expect the young life beside them to develop equally slowly. But that was no subject for discussion.

"What is your opinion," he asked, "as to Mounsey's innocence?"

"Had I a doubt of it," Morant replied, "I would not have undertaken his defence, in spite of Margot's pleas. Frederick Curtis was my friend, his brother was my partner. Their murder, if there was a murder, is a dastardly thing. The law says a man is innocent until he is proved otherwise. That is a grand maxim, the foundation of our liberty. But unless I was absolutely convinced that Wilfrid Mounsey was guiltless, I should have asked him to take the case to someone who could deal with it from a purely impersonal aspect. I believe in him. I will do my best for him."

He said it rather finely, and before Roger could reply Margot re-entered the room.

"I am ready," she said. "Wish us luck, Uncle Victor."

"I do, my dear, every possible luck. And we shall see you at dinner on Saturday, Mr. Bennion."

XI. A RAY OF HOPE

Little was said on the way to Egerton Square. Margot sat by Roger's side, meek and miserable. Only once did she start to talk.

"You think there is a chance?"

"Of course there is a chance. We may learn a lot more about Frederick Curtis before we are through."

"But there is so little to learn! I liked him; I am sorry for him; but he was so dreadfully stuffy!"

"I know what you mean, but even men like that have sides to their characters no one suspects."

"Not Frederick Curtis! He was too worried about the end of the world to have time to enjoy what there is."

"His man Foyle told us that," Roger remarked, "though he put it differently."

"I do not think Mr. Foyle can help us much. He is worse, though in another way."

"How do you mean?"

"He is so utterly dumb. We used to tease Delia about him at one time, but Mr. Foyle knows his place! Wilfrid says he has as much imagination as a balance sheet."

"There is plenty of imagination about that sometimes."

In Egerton Square the odd numbers ran along the north side and the even numbers the south. Thus No. 3 where Frederick Curtis had lived was almost faced, across the garden, by No. 6, the dwelling of Colonel Robert Parsons, D.S.O.

The Colonel was a big man with a large red face and fierce blue eyes, and he spoke in a very loud voice. But a crutch and a stick drew attention to something else. He had lost a leg in action when he gained his decoration, though he hated to be commiserated on his misfortune.

He was proud to do things for himself and could even put up a game of golf that was by no means to be despised. He was at home when Roger and Margot arrived.

"I an afraid, sir," Roger began, "we have come on rather a peculiar errand, but I hope you will let me explain. I believe you saw Wilfrid Maunsey call on his uncle Frederick Curtis on the night he was shot. In consequence of that, Mounsey has been arrested."

"Who exactly are you?" demanded the soldier, looking from him to the attractive girl by his side.

"I am only a friend. Roger Bennion is my name. This is Margot Watney who hopes to marry Wilfrid Mounsey."

The Colonel fixed his fierce blue eyes on the girl.

"I am sorry for you, young lady," he said, more gently than was his wont. "I have my duty to do, and sentiment does not came into it."

"But, please . . ." she whispered.

"I said, sir," Roger went on, "that I hoped you would let me explain. We know that what you have stated is true, but it diverges from what Mounsey says, and we are hoping it may be possible that his statement is also true."

Colonel Parsons stared at him as though wondering whether it would not be better to order him from the house.

"Please let him tell you," Margot whispered.

"I knew Curtis. He was a good fellow and whoever shot him was guilty of a damnable crime. I shall give my evidence, and I suppose I shall be cross-examined on it. It will not be pleasant, but I shall do my duty."

"I am sure of that, sir," said Roger, "but your duty would not allow you to help to condemn an innocent man and let the real criminal escape."

"What do you mean?"

"Mounsey's story is that he arrived just before half-past nine. Finding his cousin and Miss Watney were not in, he talked for a few minutes with his uncle and then left. He however remembered a little gift he had brought for Miss Watney and went back for it. It was not in his uncle's room, so he did not see him the second time and did not stay more than a minute or two. I believe you saw someone leave at about ten o'clock. If that was Wilfrid Mounsey, his story is untrue. But if it was someone else, his story may be true, and that someone else is the real murderer. So, sir, Margot Watney and I want very respectfully to ask you two questions. The first is, were you by your window all the time? The second, did you actually recognise Wilfrid Mounsey on each occasion?"

Roger had a very persuasive way with him and Colonel Parsons, despite his hectoring manner, had an honest heart. He had made one or two mildly explosive interjections, but on the whole had listened very patiently.

"You are hoping to make me say that what I told the police was untrue? That there was no shot? That it was all a mistake? I may have been a fool not to know it was a shot, but one doesn't expect things like that, and there are so many damned noises nowadays. But I tell you it was just as I said it was."

"Yes, sir. But I am asking you to consider my two questions. It was rather wet that night and if I saw a man in a hat and a mackintosh enter a house, and twenty minutes later a man in a hat and a mackintosh left it, I should assume it was the same man. But if I was not at my window all the time, and if I did not see his face on each occasion, would it not be possible for one man to go and another to arrive and for my assumption to be wrong?"

The soldier glared at him and at Margot for a few moments.

"You ought to be a lawyer," he barked, "but damme, sir, there is something in what you say. See that light over there?"

He raised himself slowly from his chair and went to the window. They followed him. He pointed to one of four lamps inside the gardens that gave them some illumination at night.

"If anyone approaches Curtis's house or my house they pass under that lamp and I can see their faces. I described the man I saw approach No. 3. He came twice, and it was Wilfrid Mounsey. I know him. I have seen him enter that way before. From my description the police recognised him and then he admitted it. There is no possible doubt about it."

"None at all, sir," agreed Roger. "But you did not see his face as he left. His back was towards you."

"What difference does that make?"

"I am only asking if it is true."

Again the colonel stared at him.

"You will make me say black is white presently. But you are right, my boy. I did not see his face when he left."

"Thank you, sir," Roger murmured quietly. "It is very good of you to say so. Were you at your window all the time?"

"I am always at my window when I am at home," barked Colonel Parsons. "It happens to be my favourite seat."

"Exactly, sir, but one sometimes gets up to attend to the fire, to alter the wireless, to get a book, or something of that sort."

"Look here, my boy, you are trying to suggest there were three arrivals and three departures and I only saw two of 'em. It won't do."

"It is not quite that, sir," said Roger. "I am only asking if it is possible you turned away from the window for just a minute or two."

"Of course I did! After the news there was a talk and then a ghastly din they call music; I remember it quite well. I stood it as long as I could, then I tuned in to Strasbourg. That is music. But don't imagine it helps you. I don't fumble with the knobs; I know what I want. I may have turned away long enough to miss young Mounsey if he left immediately, as you say he did, but not long enough for another man to arrive and go in—unless he and Mounsey met. And Mounsey admits there was no one else about."

There was a note of triumph in his voice, for which he was immediately sorry.

"Pardon me, young lady," he barked to Margot, in what he probably thought was a gentler tone. "I know how you feel, but one must face facts."

She did not reply, but Roger spoke more briskly.

"That is just the fact we wanted, sir. If Mounsey could have got away without being noticed, it makes everything easy. The other man arrived in the ordinary way by the front door. Mounsey had gone and Frederick Curtis let him in. It must have been some one Curtis knew well. When he had fired his shot and left things as he wanted them to be found, this other man decided to get out, not the way he came, but through the garden. You saw him go and naturally took him for the man you had seen enter fifteen or twenty minutes before."

The soldier's blue eyes positively bulged.

"'Pon my word, young man, you do want me to say black is white, but damme, I believe it might have been that way."

"Oh, thank you! Thank you!" murmured Margot.

"Not so much thank you, young lady! I have told my tale and I stick to it. But if it is put to me as this young feller puts it, that the second man might have arrived at the street door, and might have gone through the garden, and might have been wearing a hat and mackintosh like Mounsey wore—I won't say it was impossible."

"Hats and macs are pretty much alike on a dark night," said Roger.

"'Pon my soul, I hope you're right. I don't go back on a single word I told 'em, but if you can show it happened your way I'll be damned glad!"

"He is rather a dear," whispered Margot as they left the house. "I believe he means to help us."

"I was afraid you would kiss him," smiled Roger. "That might have been corrupting a witness. But you managed very well."

"It was all you," she said. "I could see it quite clearly in the way you put it. I am more hopeful than I have been since they took him."

"It is a start, but we still have to find the other man."

"While we are here," Margot suggested, "shall we see if Delia has heard anything?"

It was a good idea, and a moment later they were knocking at the door of No. 3. Russell, the man-servant, admitted them as Delia was at home.

"Mr. Marmaduke is with her, miss," he said to Margot, whom he knew as a frequent visitor.

"That is all right," and she pushed past him, confident of her welcome.

She opened the door of the front sitting room. Roger followed, although he would have preferred a more formal entry.

Delia and her uncle were facing one another and it was obvious they had been having something of a quarrel. The girl's fair face was flushed and she looked angry. Marmaduke was redder than usual and there was quite an ugly look in his narrow eyes.

"He wants to come and live here," cried Delia abruptly, when her friend entered the room.

"That is for you to say," commented Margot, going to her side.

"I have said!"

"It is not a matter for discussion," Marmaduke spat out, looking at the girls and then at Roger, "but if you understand the position perhaps you can make her see reason. Under her father's will I am her guardian until she is twenty-one. Therefore she must live with me. It is not possible for her to live at my chambers and that means I must take something else. Since she has this house and we should lose money if we sold it, I have decided to come here."

"I cannot have him in Daddy's place," said Delia tensely. She might not have been an ideal daughter, but she had been fond of her father. She had recovered from her first self-reproaches at his death, yet the thought of the uncle she disliked occupying his room and using the things he had used was utterly repugnant to her. Marmaduke had told her complacently of certain alterations he meant to make and had apparently been surprised at her obstinate opposition.

"I don't know much about wills," said Margot, "but it is utter rot to suggest that she will be able to look after herself in thirteen months' time but cannot now. She ran the house for her father, didn't she?"

"The law," Marmaduke declared, with more emphasis than originality, "is the law, and until a girl comes of age someone must be responsible for her."

"But the law," retorted Margot, "does not compel that someone to live with her."

"But it pleases me to live with her."

"I put it the wrong way round. She is not compelled to live with you. Plenty of girls have their allowance and live by themselves."

Marmaduke's eyes glittered dangerously.

"Their allowance may depend on how far their mode of living pleases their guardians."

"If you come here," said Delia, "I shall go."

"And what will you live on?" inquired her uncle.

To this there was no reply, and Roger ventured a word.

"Since we have intruded on a family discussion, is it permissible to inquire the general terms of the will?"

"Certainly," said Marmaduke, with some attempt at dignity. "It is far better that Delia and I should keep our feelings to ourselves, and I am quite sure on reflection she will realise I am only acting for her good. But the will is of course open to the world. Frederick made it after his wife's death and left everything to Delia; Alexander and I, or the survivor of us, being trustees and guardians. There was suitable remuneration for the duties involved."

"Delia was a kid then," Margot said warmly. "He would have done differently now."

"On the contrary," declared the uncle, "when I saw him on the day he died, he told me if anything happened to him I was to look after her."

"What time did you see him on the day he died?" Roger inquired.

Marmaduke went a deeper red.

"I do not mean the actual day," he said, "but shortly before he died."

"Was he expecting anything to happen to him?"

"I do not suppose so. It was just a general expression of his wishes, but I mean to carry them out."

He seemed to realise he had blundered, but before Roger could say anything more, Margot burst out with the news she had come to tell.

"Delia, Mr. Bennion has proved that Wilfrid didn't do it!"

"How splendid!" said Delia. "Of course he didn't, but how do you know?"

"I am afraid Margot is a bit ahead of the facts," Roger explained. "We have, I think, convinced Colonel Parsons that the man he saw leaving on the second occasion might have been someone else."

"Someone who came in at the front and went out through the garden," Margot added eagerly.

"Surmise," muttered Marmaduke scornfully. "Who was he?"

"That," said Roger, "is what we have to find out."

XII. GOFF'S DEDUCTIONS

"You have been busy while I was away," Roger said to Goff the next morning when he entered the detective's room.

"The Yard has to function whatever the difficulties."

Roger laughed. "But why only one arrest?"

"The usual reason; lack of evidence."

"You don't suspect Wilfrid Mounsey of both the crimes?"

"We do not."

"So you accept the coincidence? Two people had the urge for murder, and both fixed it for two minutes to eleven on the same night?"

"Not such a coincidence—as you showed us."

Goff was inclined to be a little short. He was a busy man and he was worried. Much as he appreciated Bennion's help in past cases and his quick notice of detail in the present ones, he had neither the time nor the inclination for discussion at large.

"So far as Mounsey is concerned," said Roger, "I have been, so to speak, retained for the defence. I thought I ought to let you know."

"By Morant?"

"No. By his niece, Margot."

"The dark girl—who wants smacking true and hard?"

"That's the one," Roger nodded cheerily.

"Anything to tell me?"

"Everything—if you will tell me something."

"Go on," grunted Goff. "No promises."

"I have seen your witness, Colonel Parsons, and he admits he was away from his window when Mounsey says he left. Away just long enough to miss him."

"But he saw him go."

"He saw someone go, fifteen minutes later. If Frederick Curtis admitted a visitor by the front door who shot him and left by the garden—how is that?"

"Quite ingenious. I won't ask who the someone was but can Mounsey account for the extra fifteen minutes? According to his landlady it was a quarter past ten when he reached his rooms, less than a mile away. He admits he walked it. If he left at ten, as Colonel Parsons says, the time just fits. If he left at a quarter to ten, as he would like us to believe, how did he fill in the time?"

"He had no reason to hurry," said Roger.

"It was a wet night."

"Dampish, not raining hard."

"Not a night for a ramble. Where did he go? What did he do?"

"He has no alibi. He was not due at the theatre until eleven and had time to kill. He probably wandered round a bit, thinking of the girl he loved and was to meet when the show was over. What are a few spots of rain to a man in that state?"

"Try it on a jury," snorted Goff, "not on me. He did not admit he had been back the second time till we proved it. Then he invented a tale about a box of chocolates, but he had lost the chocolates. And his finger-prints were on the gun."

"That is what I wanted to ask about," said Roger. "Are his prints actually on the butt of the gun and the trigger?"

"Of course not. He is not such a fool as that. He wiped the butt and the trigger and pressed his uncle's hand to 'em. But he was careless enough to hold the barrel while he did it!"

"No gloves?"

"He never wears 'em and he wouldn't need 'em. He was often in and out of the place, and his prints would be all in order—but not on the gun!"

"The only explanation we can offer for that," said Roger, "is that he handled it when they found the body."

"Or," Goff retorted, "he handled it when he smashed the watch glass. That was your idea at the start, and it is as likely now as it was then. I suppose you haven't overlooked the motive? Mounsey gets a tidy bit of money on his uncle's death, and he wants to marry this girl you are so sorry for."

"You have covered everything," Roger admitted, "and I'll own it makes a strong case. Who is the suspect for killing Alexander?"

Goff stared at him for a moment. Then he said shortly: "The so-called wife."

"Helen Curtis? It was obvious. Why is she not arrested too?"

"I cannot find how she got hold of a gun. So far as we know, Alexander Curtis never had one."

"No finger-prints there?"

"Only the dead man's. She had plenty of time."

"And apparently a lot of nerve," Roger commented. "That she could have done it is not open to doubt. Relations between them were strained, to say the least. She shot her husband and went to bed in the next room, or the next room but one, and waited for someone to bring the news in the morning. Did the maid who roused her find her awake or asleep?"

"Asleep—or so she believes. It might be pretence or dope."

"Most women in such circumstances would, I imagine, take something to make them sleep. A fairly horrible night otherwise."

Goff grunted, but said nothing.

"So," Roger went on, "we get our coincidence. Mounsey shot his uncle and put the time forward till eleven and then smashed the watch. Helen Curtis shot Alexander and put the clock back to eleven and saw that it stopped."

"Eleven," said Goff, "being as you pointed out, the exit time at theatres, the time for which each had an alibi. Mounsey was meeting his friends and the woman was with her sister. Also, no doubt, she remembered she had been speaking to Morant just then."

"It does seem obvious," Roger agreed. "There is only one trouble."

"What is that?"

"You do not quite believe it yourself. You are not happy about it."

"I get the facts. Others decide what shall be done with them."

"I know. To the normal citizen a Chief-Inspector is an awe inspiring individual, but behind the scenes there are many to whom he must bow the head."

"Plenty of 'em."

"And you would be so much happier if the facts showed that one person had engineered the whole thing."

"Trying to psycho-analyse me, or whatever they call it?" Goff demanded.

"Wouldn't dare to. Only trying to see things as I think you must. For two brothers to be shot at the same time, and for there to be no connection, wants a lot of believing."

"Wilfrid Mounsey's story wants a lot of believing, too," Goff retorted.

"It does, yet it might be true. Had there been no other crime, your case is so strong that Wilfrid might hang, innocent or not. He gets money by his uncle's death; he did not admit his second visit; he never produced the chocolates; the time he reached his rooms fits the time you say he left the house, not his time; his prints are on the gun. It looks like a true bill. Yet each point is capable of some sort of explanation, and the fact remains that another man was killed in the same way and at the same time somewhere else. The whole affair seems different from the ordinary cases you run up against."

"In what way?"

"Your murder problems—I mean those you do not solve by the usual routine—are generally in two classes. Those where someone is killed in a locked room to which apparently no one had access; and those where too many people had access—the old gentleman in the library and all his nephews and nieces and cousins and kin buzzing around in suspicious circumstances. The Curtis cases are not like either of them. There is no difficulty of approach. Both men were alone, but either might have admitted any caller. Yet, except for Helen Curtis in one case and Wilfrid Mounsey in the other, there is no evidence that anyone did call."

"I had got that far myself," said Goff dryly. "Admit that they were the only callers and what more is there?"

"The technique in both crimes was identical. Each man is shot; the wound is in the same place; and means are taken in the same way, a stopped clock or watch, to establish the time when it happened. You, with your greater experience, know even better than I do how improbable it is that Wilfrid Mounsey and Helen Curtis would have proceeded independently on such precisely similar lines."

"We have not arrested Helen Curtis," Goff replied, "and we probably shall not until we can account for her having a gun. Mounsey is different. His tale was untrue and your defence is pure surmise; Colonel Parsons might have turned away at the critical moment and might have mistaken someone else for Mounsey. Another thing. Frederick Curtis was a left-handed man and he was shot over the left ear. No casual caller would have done that. His nephew naturally knew of his peculiarity."

"I am not suggesting a casual caller," Roger rejoined. "I am convinced it was someone who knew both the brothers well; not merely because of the left-handed detail, but because they would not otherwise have been invited into the home and had the opportunity of standing so close to the victim as to make suicide plausible."

"It is a new method of defence," said Goff ironically. "Mounsey did not kill Alexander Curtis and, therefore, could not have killed Frederick, because there was similarity in the two cases. It would be just as logical for me to say he did kill Frederick, as the evidence shows and therefore he must also have killed Alexander. Instead of wandering aimlessly in the rain why should he not have gone to Sloane Square and killed the other uncle? It would just have filled in the time."

"A point to you," smiled Roger. "I want to find one person who might have done both the crimes and who had a definite motive in each case."

"So do I!" said Goff.

"Well—what about Marmaduke?"

"The third brother?"

"Yes. Have you considered him?"

"Have I not! Tell me what you know of him."

"Very little, and I have not your opportunities for checking his movements," said Roger, "but the motives are not hard to find."

"Being exactly?"

"Money. In the case of Alexander the opportunity was unique. Alexander, we hear, is a rich man. He has fallen out with his supposed wife and destroys his will. He does not make another because he is hoping to marry someone else and means maybe to settle an amount to be agreed on the supposed wife. If he dies before he does so, he dies intestate and having no legal wife his brothers share everything."

"And if the other brother dies too," suggested Goff, "Marmaduke gets the lot?"

"No. The children—or child—of the other brother inherit what could have been his."

"Marmaduke himself told us all this," remarked the detective.

"Why not? He knew you would discover it."

"Suppose you are right, suppose he and not Helen killed Alexander, it does not help young Mounsey."

"Unless we admit that both crimes were by the same hand."

"What could be Marmaduke's motive for killing Frederick, seeing that only Delia benefits?"

"On the face of it," Roger admitted, "the motive is not so strong. As Delia's guardian he will handle her money and will apparently be well paid for his trouble. Also he will be able to live for a time in the house in Egerton Square. But there may be less obvious yet more powerful reasons."

"Such as?"

"If he owed Frederick money, Frederick's death may wipe out the debt."

"Anything else?"

"If for the motive suggested he killed Alexander, he may have feared Frederick would know it. So to be safe he removed them both."

"All the maybes in the world don't make an is," said Goff.

"True. I am not accusing Marmaduke. I only asked if you had considered him. Do you remember his telling us he had not seen either of his brothers for a week before they died?"

"I do."

"Yesterday he told Delia he had spoken to her father on the day he was killed. When I asked at what time, he saw he had made a mistake and said he did not mean the actual day but a day or two before. What was Marmaduke doing on the night of the crime?"

"Up to a point," said Goff, "I can tell you. He had dinner at his club and left about 8.30. He was buying a car and had it for a few days on trial. He took it for a run and was back in the club just before eleven and had a rubber of bridge."

"Was anyone in the car with him?"

"No."

"Can he prove where he went?"

"He says he used the Kingston by-pass and went round parts of Surrey. There is no confirmation. He doesn't drink while driving, and was just putting the car through its paces."

"He could, of course, have called on either or both of his brothers and still done a bit of driving. His only alibi is for eleven—for which the clock and the watch were set."

Goff nodded. "I put it to him it was not a nice night to be out. He said greasy roads and a poor light were a better test for the brakes and lamps. And being a busy man he could not get away in the daytime."

"Is he a busy man?" queried Roger. "Have you checked up on his financial position?"

"It is not too good. But you are overlooking one thing."

"What is that?"

"You say," Goff replied, "that it was now or never for him, as directly Alexander made a will he would get nothing. But that applies even more strongly to Helen Curtis. She knew that under the old will she got everything, and she did not know the old will was destroyed. She told us so. If therefore Alexander died before he altered it, she would not only be immensely better off, but she would cut out the other woman whom she undoubtedly hated."

"But you cannot trace a weapon to her?"

"That, as I told you, is where I am stuck. Both the guns are of foreign make and are different."

"If one person did both crimes," said Roger, "he would hardly use twin pistols."

"Probably not," Goff replied. "I am glad to have had this talk with you, as you helped us a lot in the first place. Before you let sympathy for that young girl, if you don't mind my saying so, influence your judgment, Wilfrid Mounsey shot Frederick Curtis. I see no reason to doubt it. Either Helen Curtis or Marmaduke shot Alexander. I believe it was the woman, but I want to know how she got the gun. She was in Paris three months ago."

XIII. TWO WOMEN

ROGER did not feel that his call at Scotland Yard had done much to help the cause he had espoused. He would have no good news for Margot when he saw her at Ashcomb that night. The girl had got herself into a sorry plight and the case against the man she hoped to marry—and to marry soon—was not seriously shaken.

Wilfrid's finger-prints on the barrel were capable of explanation. He might have picked up the weapon unseen by the others and without conscious recollection of having done so; but would a jury accept that explanation when all the other facts were considered? It was good to get Colonel Parsons' admission that he had turned away from the window, but would that help unless it could be proved that there really had been another caller? The point lost much of its value when it had to be admitted that Wilfrid was so late in getting to his rooms.

Roger decided to make one more visit before he left town. The fate of Frederick Curtis was his immediate concern, but, unless the deaths of the two brothers were entirely independent of one another, might not the equally tragic end of Alexander throw light on what he wanted to know?

It was in many ways the more curious affair of the two. A highly respected solicitor had been "living in sin" for many years, but he took no step to break with his supposed wife until it became possible for him to marry her. He endured bonds that had become irksome so long as he felt he could break them at will. Directly it was suggested they should be made permanent, he decided to endure them no longer. Then he was killed. There are many cases on record of a man getting rid of his wife in order to marry someone else, but in this case the person got rid of was the man himself.

The one individual who might possibly solve the riddle was the woman he had desired, Dreda Costello.

It was her that Roger decided to see.

Some of the buildings near Glebe Place, Chelsea, retain much of their old-world character, and at the end of a short cul-de-sac Roger found the spot he sought.

A wide wooden door stood invitingly open and immediately inside it a flight of stairs rose steeply to the higher floor. There was a curious knocker like a death's head and with the hinged lower jaw he gave two sharp raps.

"Come up," said a voice from above.

He went up. The stairs opened directly into what had once perhaps been a loft but was now a spacious studio with an orthodox north light. It was comfortably furnished with rugs and settees, and a number of unframed paintings were hung on or leant against the walls. At the far end two doors led into what was no doubt the sleeping and domestic section.

In the centre, under the light, a woman was painting. On a stand to her left a dress of silk and lace of the rich colouring of a ripe tomato was carefully draped, and she was reproducing its folds and tints on the canvas on her easel. Her back was towards the entrance, and for some moments she continued her work without looking round. She wore long well-cut blue trousers and a white silk shirt open at the neck.

"I am afraid I am disturbing you," Roger said.

"Oh," she turned and looked at him. "I was expecting someone else."

She was a remarkable woman. Her dark hair was short and there was no attempt to dress it in any fashionable style. Her face was rather wide, but her skin and her features were good. She had no make-up of any kind. Her eyes were grey and they seemed to regard life calmly and without fear. Undoubtedly she might be beautiful if she took the trouble. Her age was probably about thirty-five. The faint smile she gave her visitor was not unfriendly.

"You have not come for your portrait?" she said.

"Is that your line?" Roger replied.

"Mostly."

"I am afraid I should not be a very interesting subject."

"Sometimes the clothes are the important part," she said, with a glance at the dress on which she had been working.

"To be immortalised in paint, one should have done something worthy of it."

"If everyone thought that artists would starve."

"There are other subjects."

"Who wants them? If I had my way, I would spend my time on vast pictures of historic scenes."

"Scotland for ever!" Roger suggested.

"The death of Julius Caesar, as I see it. Horatio on his bridge. John Knox berating Mary Queen of Scots. I was once told I had the soul of an illustrator, not an artist."

"Have you never indulged your fancy?"

"Have I never wasted my time? I have a gift for catching a likeness, so I paint a dress and add the commonplace but opulent features afterwards!"

"I could send my golf suit," said Roger.

Again she smiled.

"What nonsense we are talking. Why have you come?"

"It is rather a personal, perhaps an impertinent matter," he said. "But a man's life may depend on it."

"Sit down."

"Won't you have a cigarette?"

She took one and sat on one of the settees. He continued to stand.

"The brothers Alexander and Frederick Curtis were both shot on the same night. It appeared to be suicide, but there are reasons in both cases for thinking it was not."

"Go on," she said quietly.

"Wilfrid Mounsey, nephew of Frederick Curtis, has been arrested for shooting his uncle. The girl he is to marry is convinced of his innocence, and for her sake I am trying to discover the truth. Did you know Frederick Curtis?"

"I have heard of him. I never met him."

"You knew his brother Alexander?"

"I did."

She spoke calmly, her eyes looking straight into his.

"Do you believe he committed suicide?"

"I do not."

"Have you any idea as to who may have killed him?"

Dreda looked at him for some moments in her cool appraising manner.

"I think," she said, "before we go further, you should tell me who you are and why you have come to me."

"I should have introduced myself," he replied, with his really charming smile, "but we started our talk a little unorthodoxly. I am Roger Bennion. I was brought into the case first by my friend Inspector Goff. Perhaps you have seen him?"

"I have."

"My interest was, in a way, the study of coincidence. But I met Margot Watney and Wilfrid Mounsey, and when Wilfrid was arrested I thought a mistake had—or might have been—made."

"Yes?"

"I came to you because I was present when Goff heard of your friendship with Alexander Curtis."

"And how," she said slowly, still looking very straight at him, "can my friendship with Alexander Curtis affect the question whether or not Wilfrid Mounsey shot Frederick Curtis?"

"Because I think the same person was guilty of both the crimes. It has been suggested that Helen Curtis might have shot Alexander but not Frederick, and Wilfrid Mounsey might have shot Frederick but not Alexander. If one person was responsible for both the deaths then those two are innocent."

Again she regarded him in her calm, steady way.

"I thought," she said quietly, "that both the deaths were supposed to have happened at the same time, about eleven o'clock?"

"That was the implication—which probably shows that neither actually happened then."

"I am afraid I cannot tell you who could have shot them both."

"Can you tell me who might have shot Alexander?"

Dreda stubbed out her cigarette and shook her head when he offered another. "I do not think it was Helen."

"Do you suspect anyone else?"

"I do not. I am completely baffled."

There was a pause. Then she went on, in the same quiet way: "I suppose you were told that Alexander wanted to marry me?"

"I was. I take it it was true?"

"Quite true. I am not a home-wrecker. I would not come between a husband and wife, or even between people who were living together if they were reasonably happy. But when their life is hell, need it continue?"

Roger made no answer.

"It was because she had no legal hold on him that Helen held him so tight. Alexander was a fine man, and he was made that way. It was pity rather than love that attracted her to him in the first place. He was sorry for her and he was indignant at her being chained for all time to a lunatic who had misused her. I do not suppose there is much knight-errantry in most lawyers, but there was a bit of it in Alexander. It soon proved that pity is a poor thing on which to build happiness. You may be terribly sorry for a woman whose husband beats her, but that does not show that she and you will be happy together. It proves you have a kind heart, not that she is a good companion."

"Helen was not a good companion?" Roger murmured.

"Her tastes and Alexander's were totally different. He loved quiet, she loved noise. He was fond of books, music and pictures. She was only happy in a crowd. A night at home with him bored her to distraction. Yet he had taken her, and to him the obligation was almost more binding than marriage would have been. She understood that, and she played upon it. He had had the best years of her life; she had left all in her trust for him—that sort of thing. I do not believe he would ever have broken the chains had she been content to leave them as they were, the bonds of his own making. But when she determined to forge them into the legal fetters of marriage he became equally determined to be free of them. Do you think that is understandable?"

She had been speaking in the low even voice of one who had come to certain conclusions after due and careful thought.

"It is perfectly understandable," Roger replied.

"I want you to realise the sort of man he was. He had definitely decided to break with Helen, but still I do not think she caused his death. She might have been capable of it in one of her outbursts of anger and of self-pity, but I do not believe she could I have planned the elaborate pretence of suicide and then stayed in the flat till it was discovered."

"But you are convinced the suicide was a pretence?"

"Absolutely," said Dreda.

She paused a moment, as though considering whether or not to say what was in her mind.

"You might not think it from the books and films of to-day, but there are probably more people than is generally supposed to whom the sex impulse means very little. They want companionship, not the gratification of desire. It was that way with Alexander. It is that way with me. He had sought no other woman when Helen failed him, and men are not essential to me. He and I met, and almost from the first our understanding was wonderful. There is just one thing I can tell you that possibly may help."

Again she paused. Again he waited.

"You will remember the death happened on a Friday night. A week from yesterday. That Friday I went to the Isle of Wight. He was to have come with me for the week-end. Please do not put the usual interpretation on the words. I might not have denied him what he wanted had he wanted it, but he did not. We should have enjoyed our few days together, but they would have been what is called innocent. He wished to marry me, but he was too great a gentleman to think of anything else."

Roger believed her. Her quiet tones carried conviction. Too great a gentleman. That perhaps had been Alexander's trouble. It was a fine epitaph.

"He did not go with you," was his comment.

"He telephoned me that he was unable to do so, as he was expecting to see someone on a matter of great importance."

"At his home?"

"That was what he said."

"Then he did have another caller?"

"I imagine so."

"He did not suggest who it was, or what was the nature of the business?"

"No. It seemed to worry him, but he said he would be coming down on the Saturday, and I did not ask any questions."

"You told this to Inspector Goll?"

"I did. He replied that they could get no confirmation of such a call."

"Anyone knowing the flats could probably slip upstairs unobserved," said Roger.

It was indeed an important point. Goff had not mentioned it, but possibly it accounted for his reluctance to arrest Helen, apart from the question of her having a weapon.

"We know that Alexander's partner Mr. Morant gave him tickets for the theatre," Roger added. "Perhaps he passed them on to Helen in order that she should be out when the visitor came."

"Probably," Dreda agreed. "Or the call might have concerned his arrangements with Helen; he was very anxious to get things settled. But in either case it would not help you in showing Wilfrid Mounsey did not shoot Frederick."

"It might, if I could show that Frederick also had a caller, especially if it was the same caller."

"But I do not think Frederick knew anything about me."

"Do you know the other brother, Marmaduke?"

"I have met him."

Dreda spoke coldly. Roger judged she had no enthusiasm for the surviving brother and little inclination to discuss him.

"Please remember," he said earnestly, "I am not here for idle gossip."

"If I thought that," Dreda returned, "I would have asked you to go at once."

"Can Marmaduke have been Alexander's caller?"

"It is quite possible, yet . . ."

"What?" asked Roger bluntly, as she paused.

"Had it been Marmaduke, why should Alexander not have said so?"

"He only told you it was a matter of business?"

"Yes. He knew I disliked Marmaduke and that may have been why he did not mention his name."

"Did they have business together?"

"Are not brothers almost sure to have some dealings with one another?"

"You do not care to tell me about it?"

Dreda's level brows contracted in a frown.

"It is not exactly that," she said in her deliberate way. "I do not want my prejudices to mislead me—or you."

"You want Alexander's murderer to be caught?"

"Indeed I do!"

"But you hesitate to suggest it may have been Marmaduke?"

"I told you I disliked Marmaduke. I mistrust him. He knew about Helen and about me, and was always wanting to know what our plans were. I resented his interference, but Alexander said it was only a desire to be helpful."

"He had Alexander's confidence?" Roger asked.

"Unfortunately he had. He tried to gain mine, but I avoided him. I felt he posed as a friend for the sheer joy of dabbling in other people's troubles."

"There are folk like that. You know that he benefits by Alexander's death?"

"You mean because of that loan?" Dreda enquired.

"I was not aware of any loan," said Roger. "I mean that so far as we know Alexander died intestate and so half his estate would go to Marmaduke."

"What about Helen?"

"Since she was not his wife she would get nothing."

"But that is terrible," Dreda exclaimed. "Alexander never meant that. Cannot anything be done about it?"

"That would depend on the good feeling of the family."

"The good feeling of Marmaduke!"

"Yes, Marmaduke. Delia's share could not be touched while she is under age. Marmaduke apparently is her trustee."

"I must see him," said Dreda. "He must do something for Helen."

Roger admired the way in which she thought of the other woman. She herself would get nothing. No doubt she was in a measure independent, but death had robbed her not only of a husband but of affluence. She gave the impression of one who could fight her own battles.

There was a pause. Then the other aspect of her case returned to her mind.

"Is it your suggestion," she asked, "that Marmaduke called on Alexander and shot him because he could inherit half his estate if he died without making a will?"

"We have no proof that Marmaduke did call," Roger answered! "If he did, the motive would seem to justify the suspicion."

"But Frederick was shot too. No such motive could apply there."

"Inspector Goff is willing to believe in coincidence— that the crimes happened at the same time but were not connected with one another. I am looking for the connection. You said Marmaduke borrowed money from Alexander. Was it much?"

"Alexander never talked about it. I knew of it from a remark he made one day. I judged it was about five thousand pounds."

"Had Marmaduke also borrowed from Frederick?"

"It is not improbable," said Dreda. "Marmaduke is a toady, quite unlike the others. But I know nothing of his dealings with Frederick. If he borrowed from him there would be some record of it, wouldn't there?"

"Not necessarily, between brothers. And the record, if any, might pass into Marmaduke's hands as trustee."

"And he could destroy it?"

Before Roger could reply there was a noise on the stairs below.

"Here is your belated friend," he said.

"Come up," Dreda called.

There was a heavy step and a moment later a form appeared in the open doorway. But it was not the person either of them could have expected.

It was Helen Curtis.

For a moment the two women confronted one another. Neither spoke. Helen, in the black trappings of widowhood, looked flushed and angry. Dreda, in the workmanlike attire of her calling, remained cool and almost expressionless. Roger said nothing; he felt that no good could come from such a strange encounter.

Then Helen flung on the floor an unfastened packet of letters and envelopes. They scattered in all directions, envelopes and letters separated as though to give the idea—no doubt intentionally—that the contents of the communications had been read.

"Yours!" said Helen. "I thought you had better have them. Poor stuff!"

She spoke with deliberate rudeness. Her flushed face suggested she had primed herself with drink for what she meant to do. A spot of colour mounted Dreda's cheeks, but she retained her self-control.

"If that is all," she said quietly, "perhaps you will go."

"It is not all. There are these."

Helen drew from her bag two faded flowers and a menu card, a pair of cuff-links and a small book, and she threw them on the floor among the letters. She also produced a photograph of Dreda. She looked at it with contempt, tore it in four pieces, and cast them down with the rest.

"If you claim anything else," she said insolently, "you had better let me know before Marmaduke takes it."

It was obvious that no kind thought prompted her actions. She hoped to humiliate her rival by showing that her secrets were known.

"Please go," said Dreda.

"I will go, but there is just this. You tried to steal him from me, but he preferred shooting himself to being with you! You are the most contemptible—"

"Stop!" said Roger.

He went to the door and opened it more widely.

Helen turned her anger on him.

"You are here! You are with the police! Perhaps you can tell me why I am followed wherever I go? Why one of your spies always hangs outside the flats? I suppose I have been followed here. That is partly why I came. A rare jest to lead them to that woman!"

"I am not from the police," said Roger, "but I think you had better go."

Quiet as were his words, there was something grim in his eye. "I wouldn't stay with that slut," she said, and she went unsteadily down the stairs. A moment later they heard the door close behind her.

"I am sorry," said Roger a little awkwardly. "Can I help pick these up?"

He pointed to the litter on the floor. Dreda shook her head.

"I would sooner you went," she said. "You see what Alexander was up against? Brandy."

"Often?"

"I am afraid so. But I do not think she shot him."

He murmured words of good-bye, but she did not heed them. She was on her knees gathering up her notes of affection and good will for the man she had lost. A middle-aged romance perhaps. She had shed no tears. She would still face the world as bravely as of old, but there was a wound in her heart that time would never wholly heal.

Roger made yet one more call; to see Gordon Lisle. Then he was free for his week-end visit.

XIV: THE LAWYER AT HOME

ASHCOMB was the sort of place estate agents would describe as a gem, and they would do so with more than usual justification. It was surrounded by woodlands, and of its own acres, intersected by a bubbling stream, two were taken up by a lake beautifully fringed with willows and lofty rhododendrons. The lawns were perfect, there was every variety of flowering tree and shrub, and the gardens had been so planned that each turn in the winding path ways revealed new and unexpected beauties. The hydrangea walk with its masses of gorgeous colour, toning from vivid crimson to the deepest blue, was perhaps its greatest glory.

The house, on a slight eminence, was built of stone, but was so covered with glowing creeper and wistaria that except for its mullioned windows very little of its actual structure could be seen. It had only a dozen bedrooms, but most of them possessed its own bathroom. Victor Morant undoubtedly had an eye for comfort, yet there was nothing ostentatious about the place or its furnishings. It sought to be good, not showy; and it succeeded.

Roger Bennion was duly appreciative when he arrived on the Saturday afternoon. As one whose job it was to make out-of-date residences convenient and attractive, he was able to recognise the good work of others. He was heartily welcomed by his host, who invited him to have a whisky and soda, and said after that Margot could show him the gardens, if he cared to see them.

"She has been terribly anxious for you to come, poor girl," Mr. Morant went on. "I hope you have good news for her. She is very distressed about young Mounsey."

"Not as good as I would have wished," Roger replied, "though enough to be hopeful."

"I am glad of that. We will not discuss it now, if you don't mind. I am expecting other guests at any moment and I have a lot to do for my meeting to-night. To-morrow we shall not be interrupted. Have you ever met Lotta Denys?"

"The actress?" Roger asked.

"The principal lady in this play in which I am interested. She is coming down tomorrow, so we had better have our talk in the morning. When she arrives I am afraid she will keep us all in attendance on her." He smiled whimsically, and added, "A great pleasure, of course."

Then Margot joined them. She wore a simple linen frock and a large shady hat. She really looked charming, although Roger could not fail to see the questioning anxiety in her eyes.

"You might show Mr. Bennion the gardens, my dear," said her uncle. "Perhaps he would like a swim before dinner."

Roger did not linger over his drink. He could see Margot longed for his news and, scanty as it was, he did not wish to keep her waiting.

"Let us go to the lake," she said, when they left the house. "It is quiet there."

They went along in silence. There were signs everywhere of the unremitting toil that it takes to make and keep up a garden, but except for one old fellow who touched his hat respectfully, and who lived in a cottage in the grounds, there was no one about. Saturday brings rest. To the week-end visitor all was charming, with no sign of effort or of labour. It is not until one actually starts the unending war with weeds and pests, until one's own back aches with the hoeing and the mowing, the pruning and manuring, that one fully realises the truth that gardens are not made by sighing "Oh, how beautiful," and sitting in the shade!

"Have you the green thumb?" Roger asked.

"I love the garden," Margot said shortly, "but I don't do any thing in it."

"A big job to keep it all as beautiful as this."

"We have three men."

Nothing more was said until they reached a seat near the bathing hut at the edge of the lake. They sat down and the girl whispered her eager question.

"Have you been able to do anything?"

"Not a great deal." He told her of his activities since he had seen her the day before. "Perhaps the most hopeful discovery is that Alexander was expecting a visitor and that is why he stayed at home."

"How does that help Wilfrid?"

"If Alexander did not shoot himself and was waiting for a caller, the same may be true of Frederick. Something was happening to one of the brothers that we do not know about, and it may be the other brother was equally concerned."

"How can we find out?"

"Can Delia help us? Has she really considered all possibilities from that point of view?"

"I am sure she has. She wants to help. She believes in Wilfrid, but she is as lost as we are."

Margot sounded despondent. It was not surprising. A few moments later she asked:

"Did you advertise about the chocolates?"

"I did. What do you think of this?"

He handed her a slip of paper with the paragraph that had appeared in several daily journals that morning.

'Five pounds reward. A box of chocolates was left in a taxi near Charing Cross on Friday, July 14, at about 11 p.m. The above reward will be paid on the return of the empty box or on proof of what happened to it. Address X.Y.Z.'

"My friend Gordon Lisle," Roger added, "is on the staff of a Sunday paper that specialises in crime. To-morrow he will quote the advertisement and tell something of its inner meaning. He will hint that it concerns an alibi for a man accused of a serious crime and will say the finder has nothing to fear by telling his story. Lisle will make quite a splash of it. We ought to hear something."

"Would it not be better to describe the box?" suggested Margot. "They were Daydream chocolates, a one pound box. There was a picture of a Cairn terrier on the lid and it had an orange ribbon bow at the corner. Wilfrid remembered that afterwards; those are the chocolates he always gives me."

"That would not do at all," said Roger. "The finder must be able to produce the actual box or describe it, otherwise it would prove nothing."

"But there may be others like it?"

"I do not doubt there are. At one time chocolate boxes were adorned with the faces of pretty girls, but the fashion has changed. Now dogs and landscapes are more popular. Of course each design is repeated scores or hundreds of times, but it is hardly likely that two Cairn terrier boxes were left in taxis in the Strand on the same night."

"If you get it, will it prove his story is true?" she asked rather pathetically.

"It will be a big help," Roger assured her. "Don't be down-hearted. We will find the truth sooner or later. We have not the resources of Scotland Yard, but Gordon Lisle has promised me the aid of some of his bright young lads if we need them. Of course he hopes for sensational copy, and he will probably get it when we are through."

The dinner guests were Major and Mrs. Cope, and Dr. and Mrs. Walling. Local residents of some importance, they were to support Mr. Morant at his evening meeting, Major Cope being the chairman. The ladies had no very distinctive characteristics and were very silent except when opportunity offered to eulogise their host for his benefactions to the neighbourhood. The talk for the most part had a political tendency and Roger, although interested, did not air his opinions. Margot got through her duties as hostess quite creditably but her uncle and his two friends largely monopolised the conversation.

"I am not too sure about this capital levy of yours, Morant," said Dr. Walling. "I support you because I think we want more men of independent views in Parliament. A thing is not necessarily right because a Conservative proposes it, and not necessarily wrong because it comes from Labour. I say every motion should be considered on its merits whoever brings it forward."

He glanced round the table as though he had expressed a strikingly new and boldly revolutionary opinion.

"Besides," added his wife, "what would have happened to our blanket fund last winter without Mr. Morant's support?"

"The wireless you gave to the village hall," said Mrs. Cope, beaming on her host, "has been wonderfully appreciated, but I don't care for some of the music, do you?"

Her husband, the Major, frowned at her. Who wanted to talk about music? "I think the capital levy is right," he said emphatically, "and I shall tell 'em so. It will mean a lower income tax, and that is what we want, especially on pensions. A man serves his country for the greater part of his life and is promised a pension when he retires. Does he get it? No! They knock off a quarter or more for tax. Is that British justice?" He in turn glared round the table.

"What do you say to that, Mr. Bennion?" asked Mr. Morant with something of a twinkle in his eye.

"I am all for abolishing income tax and every other tax," said Roger, "but how it is to be done I have come here to learn."

The others elaborated their proposals and it was some time before there was any reference to the matter in which he was really interested.

"I was rather afraid," said Dr. Walling to his host, "that you might have to postpone the meeting when I heard of the tragic death of your partner, Mr. Curtis."

"And his brother was killed too," added Mrs. Cope., "I see they have arrested his nephew. What a terrible thing!"

"I did think of cancelling the meeting," said Mr. Morant, "but I felt one's duty to the public should come before one's private feelings."

"A very fine sentiment," Major Cope pronounced. "I shall tell 'em so."

The village hall was full when they arrived and there was immediate evidence of Mr. Morant's popularity. How far it was due to agreement with his proposals and how far it was influenced by gratitude for his benefactions— especially that gratitude that has been defined as a lively sense of favours to come—cannot be determined. But a speaker who can offer to cure all the ills from which his hearers suffer; low wages, high prices and unemployment, by a remedy for which others will have to pay, is generally sure of a good hearing.

After he had been introduced by his chairman, Mr. Morant expounded the views he had already explained to Roger and Inspector Goff. He spoke well and he made a very impressive figure on the platform. He said he had no use for party politics, he wanted to see general well-being and prosperity for all.

"What is it that stands in the way?" he demanded. "It is debt. The debt that has our country in its clutches and is slowly but surely choking out its life.

"Commercial concerns sometimes find themselves in difficulty. What is their remedy? They must reconstruct, or in other words write off their liabilities. That is what our country must do. A sweeping tax on capital is the only way to health and liberty. Not an annual tax, but one big levy that will wipe out our debts and give us a new start. Operations are generally painful. For some of us this operation will be painful. It will be painful for me. But our children and our children's children will reap the benefit. Instead of inheriting a crushing despairing burden of misery and debt, they will be born free; free to enjoy the fruits of their labours, not to spend their years in hopeless toil to pay for the follies of their forefathers."

There was a good deal of applause when he sat down. The chairman asked for questions and these were soon forthcoming.

"If wealth were all in cash," said a man, evidently a farmer, "'twould be easy enough. But what would happen when 'tis in land and cattle and machines?"

"Everything would be valued," Mr. Morant explained, "and above a certain figure a share would be taken in cash or in kind."

"Who would do the valuing?" asked someone else. "Would all our sticks be valued? How long would it take?"

"Most people have insurance policies. They might be a basis of valuation. It would hardly effect small householders."

"The value of a thing," said another, "is what it will fetch. What will anything fetch if we all have to sell at the same time?"

"If I lose part o' my land," added the farmer who had spoken first, "I get rid of some o' the men. How will that cure unemployment or feed the men's children?"

"Order! Order!" rapped the chairman. "One at a time, please."

"I've gotten a bit by the sweat o' my brow," said an old fellow in front. "You say 'twon't be touched, but how do 'ee know? Once start pilfering, where wil't end?"

This was applauded. Morant smiled, and asked for more.

"Woan't gov'ment never want to borrow again? Who will lend to a thief?" This came from another farmer.

"We want more rich people, not more poor ones," shouted a voice.

Then several started to speak at the same time and the chairman hammered on his table till there was quiet.

"Your comments," said Mr. Morant, with his charming smile, "are, as I would expect, both interesting and intelligent. It would take another long speech to answer them all and I am sure you do not want that. It is a big scheme and I did not say there would be no hardships. I said quite the reverse. But land does not go out of cultivation because it changes hands. The new owner will want new workers. Remember thousands of millions of debt have to be paid off. Is it not better to do it in one painful operation than to have years and generations of misery and despair? For my part I think it is, and I believe most of you agree with me."

He sat down. The chairman started to sing "He's a jolly good fellow," and most of the audience joined in right lustily. Then a photographer took a flashlight picture for the local journal and the meeting dispersed.

"What did you think of it all?" Mr. Morant asked Roger as they were driven back to Ashcomb in his luxurious car. Margot had not come with them.

"I think," smiled Roger, "you will get a lot of supporters when the time comes, though whether they understand the working of your scheme is another matter."

"Do you believe in it?"

"I am no politician, but I think there was a lot in what your questioners said."

"It is the only alternative to state ownership. I am a rich man and you are a rich man, or your father is. Take away half our possessions, and we should soon be as rich again, for we have the gifts that make for success. Wipe out the nations' debts, and those who have no such gifts will have a chance to live decently."

"I must study the subject," said Roger, declining to be drawn into argument.

"I am tired," admitted Morant, as the car completed its short journey. "These affairs are very exhausting. We will talk to morrow."

XV. LOTTA DENYS

"Look!" said Margot. "Your friend has made a fine show of it." She produced a copy of the News of the People and pointed to Roger's advertisement printed in big type across two columns under the heading, "Five Pounds For an Empty Chocolate Box!"

Gordon Lisle had kept his promise. Below the advertisement it said:

"Many must have seen this announcement in yesterday's papers and wondered what it meant. We could tell them, but we may not do so, as it concerns a case that is sub judice.

"When we say it is a Murder Case and perhaps the most sensational Murder Case of the decade, our readers will realise its grim importance. It is no stunt advertisement to boost a particular brand of chocolates as some may have thought. We do not know—we do not care—what sort of chocolates were in that box. This we will say: A man has given a certain statement to the police as to his movements on the night in question. He says he was in the Strand just before 11 p.m. on the Friday night and left a box of chocolates in a taxicab. The driver has been traced, but he knows nothing of the chocolates. He however says he had three more fares immediately afterwards. One of them probably found the chocolates. If so they are asked to explain the circumstances. There is no question of blame for misappropriation. If the box, or adequate proof of its existence at the time, can be brought to us, we will guarantee the payment of the reward.

"Remember! A man's life may depend on it!"

"I see Lisle has not put the Postal Box number," Roger remarked. "He hopes the party concerned will go to him."

"Good journalese," said Mr. Morant. "When did the advertisement appear?"

"In yesterday's morning papers."

"You do not waste time."

"You might get a reply to-morrow," said Margot.

"Several, probably," observed her uncle. "I do not want to disappoint you, my dear, but even if we get the actual chocolates, I am afraid it does not prove much."

"It proves Wilfrid's story is true!" she cried.

"It proves he had a box of chocolates, but it does not prove it was to fetch them that he paid his second visit to his uncle's house. Counsel on the other side may argue that it is equally consistent with their theory. He did not mention his second visit until they heard of it from Colonel Parsons. If he were guilty of the crime they allege, it would account for a state of agitation that would cause him to leave his chocolates in his cab."

"But he was not agitated," the girl insisted. "I can vouch for that, so can the others."

"That is a point we will not forget," said Mr. Morant. "Have you learnt anything else?"

Roger told him of his talk with Dreda Costello and of the visitor Alexander Curtis was expecting. He did not mention the call from Helen Curtis. He had not said anything about that to Margot.

"Interesting," commented the lawyer, "but it does not help us much. That Alexander had an unknown caller does not show that Frederick had one too."

"But it encourages us to go on," said Roger. "If Wilfrid's story is true, as we believe it to be, Frederick must have had another caller. Colonel Parsons' admission that he left his window allows for his being mistaken as to the second man he saw go away. Both the brothers were murdered. If one of them had a visitor on some mysterious errand it makes it more probable the other had the same visitor on the same errand."

"Yes," said Mr. Morant slowly, "it is a good theory. I wish we could get more facts."

"Do you know anything of Marmaduke's financial dealings with his brothers?"

The lawyer looked at him sharply, but did not immediately reply.

"Were there such dealings?" he asked after a pause.

"I thought you might be able to tell me," Roger replied.

"My partner had an opinion of his brother Marmaduke that I did not share. It was one of the few things in which we did not see eye to eye. I believe he lent him money. Why do you ask?"

"Miss Costello puts the loan at five thousand pounds. She also thinks Marmaduke borrowed from Frederick. There may be no proof of the facts now the lenders are dead."

"You are suggesting that Marmaduke was the unknown caller in each case, and that he shot both his brothers?"

"I am asking what you think of such a possibility," said Roger. "In the case of Alexander, he knew there was no will, and it was much to his advantage if he died without making one."

"I do not like Marmaduke," answered Mr. Morant gravely, "but I should hesitate to accept so terrible a proposition without the strongest support. I can only wish you every success in your efforts, whatever their result and whoever may be implicated. We are seeking for justice. If your advertisements bring any replies, you may, if you wish, send the parties to me."

Mr. Morant was right in saying serious talk would be impossible when Lotta Denys arrived. She was a fascinating young Frenchwoman and was not content unless all the men in sight were paying her adequate attention. She had no rival that after noon as Margot was content to be alone. Her court was a small one; only Mr. Morant and Roger and a man named Frank Rudway who had motored her down. He was Mr. Morant's general manager at the theatre and had produced his latest play.

In the circumstances Lotta's battery of pouts and smiles and languishing glances was directed mainly at Roger, he being the only possible new victim. She certainly had wonderful eyes and her soft voice, with a little gurgle of laughter in it, had made her a great favourite with the playgoing public.

She was of course capricious, and Mr. Morant seemed only too pleased to satisfy her whims. She at first ordained that everyone should bathe in the lake before lunch, but when they had changed and she had revealed herself in the daintiest and most fragmentary of costumes, she decided otherwise. She donned a striking wrap in pale blue and mauve and said they would have lunch in the shade by the side of the water. Orders were given accordingly.

Roger was introduced, and she soon got busy with him, apparently to the annoyance of both her host and Frank Rudway.

"What do your friends call you?" she asked.

"Roger," he said, recognising the opening.

"Rogaire—I like the name Rogaire. It is really a man's name. I had a vairy dear friend once who was called Rogaire." Her smile insinuated that another Roger might be equally dear.

"What is so manly about the name Roger?" asked Mr. Morant. "Chaucer's cook is called Roger. 'He could roast, seethe, broil and fry. Make porridge and well bake a pie.' Not exactly masculine attributes."

"There is the Black Roger," said Rudway morosely, "the symbol of piracy."

"Generally called the Jolly Roger," laughed the owner of the name. "As a matter of fact, it originally meant famous with the spear."

"Yet not always the Victor," smiled Mr. Morant.

"Probably not always Frank," said Rudway.

"Ah, Veector, Frank, Rogaire, I love them all," gurgled Lotta. "You have seen my new play—yes?" This again was to Roger.

"Not yet. I am not one of those important people who are invited to first nights, so I prefer to wait three or four weeks till a play settles into its stride."

"If it lasts so long," added Rudway gloomily.

"Of course it will last so long," said Lotta. "There was a good house last night. They loved it."

"Paper." Rudway's lips formed the word, but did not say it aloud.

From what he had read of the play Roger was not particularly anxious to see it. It was designed to afford Lotta the fullest display of her coquetries, but the plot was just that of one of the bedroom farces of fifty years ago. The pretty wife of the elderly and jealous husband had invited her dear friend to visit her in his absence, but being in bed with an alleged cold said he might peep into her room for just a moment. The maid by a mistake showed the wrong man in—dear friend number two, secretary to number one. Then number one arrives, and number two hides under the bed or Madame will be compromised. Number three of course also comes, so number two, equally of course, hides in the wardrobe. Then comes the husband, and number three has to pose as a doctor. The husband, alarmed at his wife's illness, urges the "doctor" to sound her chest. There is a sneeze from under the bed. The husband, who is not looking, believes it was his wife and says he will get a wrap from the wardrobe. The wife jumps out of bed to stop him. . . . It was all very funny the first time it was done. Lotta's keenest admirers had to regret the author had not found something a little newer for her.

"I have been told," Roger was saying, "the second night is often the worst. It has not the thrill of a first night, and the actors, having read all the criticisms, with their probably conflicting opinions, are not so sure of themselves."

"Ah, that sec-cond night," said Lotta, raising her hands, "it was ter-ri-ble!"

"You need not have pinched Freddie's lines," Rudway muttered.

"How was that?" asked Mr. Morant.

"In the second act," explained Rudway, "when Mangrol arrives, Freddie says, 'If he catches me here I am undone.' Lotta tells him to get under the bed. He sticks, so she tells him to take off his coat and waistcoat. He does, and then, as you know, he catches his braces and they break. He says, 'Now indeed I am undone.' Not brilliant, but it got a laugh the first night. Lotta pinched it, but she said, 'Now indeed you are unfastened.' It not only fell flat but it put Freddie out of his stride."

"It was not my fault," protested Lotta. "We had been changing and chopping all day as to what we should say and who should say it, and I thought that was right. What is the difference between unfastened and undone?"

"No difference—sometimes," said Mr. Morant. "It was all right the next night?"

"Oh, yes," said Rudway. "She got no laugh, so she kept to her lines."

"Frankie dear," murmured Lotta, "sometimes I think I hate you. You try to make Rogaire believe I am greedy, when all I care for is the success of the show. Do people come to see Freddie or to see me, Lotta Denys? So I give them all I can."

"Whether it is your own or his," muttered Rudway.

So the day slipped away; sunning, swimming, flirting, quarrelling. Roger at one time had a few quiet words with Rudway, whom he was inclined to like.

"Will the play pull through?" he asked.

Rudway shrugged. "I doubt it."

"But Lotta is charming."

"Very charming—when she does as she is told. Morant lets her have her way in everything and that means no one else gets a look in. Half the actors and actresses in London would ruin every play they appear in if they had the chance. They want to say all the juicy lines themselves. Lotta is clever, but it needs a good producer to give just the right amount of her stuff and no more. Otherwise another flop."

"Mr. Morant has not been lucky?"

"This will be the third failure in six months, It doesn't matter to him—just a hobby, he can afford it, but it does a lot of harm to some of us. And I could make Lotta go a long way if she would only listen."

Roger left early the next morning. It had been a pleasant experience in its way, but he felt that so far as helping Wilfrid Mounsey was concerned it had been time wasted. He was rather surprised when Mr. Morant asked him to come again the following week-end.

"I have not been able to give you much time," he said, "but I shall think over all you have told me and in the meanwhile a lot may happen. I know Margot would like you to come if you can."

"Can you?" asked the girl, who was with them.

Roger felt he had not been much comfort to her in the tragedy she was facing. He wished she had a woman in whom she could confide. Dreda Costello, who was bearing her own loss so bravely, might have been a comfort to her. But he did not like to suggest it.

"You will be in town during the week?" he asked.

"I expect so," she said. "If there is anything I can do, please let me know. I cannot sleep for thinking of Wilfrid in such misery."

"Try not to think of it, my dear," said her uncle. "He will be all right, won't he, Bennion?"

"I hope so," Roger replied. "No doubt I shall be communicating with you both, especially if our advertisement brings any replies, so we might see how things develop."

XVI. THE CHOCOLATE BOX

WHEN Roger reached London his first step was to telephone Gordon Lisle to ask if there had been any response to his chocolate box campaign in the "crime weekly."

"Response!" echoed his friend. "A sackful, and still pouring in. One would imagine that leaving chocolates in taxis was a national hobby. Lots of course are fakes, but a few seem genuine and worth looking into. Did your advertisement bring any answers?"

"I don't know yet," Roger replied. "I am on my way to the agency to find out."

"Don't forget to tell me of anything good."

"I won't."

The office to which replies were to be sent had only three letters for him. The first was obviously a "try on." Mr. John Smith, writing from an accommodation address, said that if the advertiser would describe the box of chocolates, he had no doubt at all it would tally with one in his possession, found in the circumstances described.

"Or he will soon get one that does," Roger muttered.

The other two notes appeared more hopeful, and both, curiously enough, came from Maida Vale.

One said that the writer had found a box of chocolates at about 11 p.m. in the Strand on the night in question, not in a taxicab, but at the edge of the pavement. She would be happy to show the empty box to the advertiser if he cared to call and she hoped it would be what he was looking for. The note was signed G. Sherlot (Mrs.).

That did not look too bad. It was possible that Wilfrid Mounsey had dropped his chocolates in the gutter and not left them in the cab. It was also possible that G. Sherlot

(Mrs.) had found them in the cab but, knowing she ought not to have walked off with them, preferred to say they had been on the pavement. It would be well to see her.

The remaining note was more intriguing. It came from an address in Lauderdale Mansions.

'Will the £5 be paid to the person what found the chocolates, or to the person what has the box and can restore same?

Yours respectful, Ada White.'

Roger felt sanguine about this reply and the event proved he was right.

He called first on Mrs. Sherlot. She was a pleasant woman and there was no reason to doubt her story. She said she had seen someone drop a box of chocolates, but by the time she had retrieved it, its owner was swallowed up in a crowd emerging from a theatre. But it was not the Jollity Theatre and the chocolates were not Daydreams, so that was no help.

At the Lauderdale Mansions flat the door was opened by a yellow-haired girl with a pert, cockney face.

"Can I see Miss Ada White?" asked Roger politely.

"If yer sight's good."

"You are Miss White?"

"I am."

"It is about this letter. May I come inside?"

"Well, what about it?" Ada White admitted him and closed the door.

"You suggest that you have the box, but you were not the actual finder?"

"That's right. Do I get the five pounds?"

"Suppose you first show me the box."

She stared at him suspiciously for a moment. Then she went along a little passage and returned with some object behind her back.

"What about the quids?" she said.

Roger showed his well-filled note-case and then imitated her action, putting it behind him.

"What about the box?"

"Is this it?"

She held out what undoubtedly might have been it. A box of Daydream chocolates, one pound size, with the picture of a Cairn terrier and having a bow of orange-coloured silk on the corner.

"That is it, or its twin," said Roger quietly, though he felt a thrill of excitement. "Do you read the News of the People?"

"Wish we did. We 'ave the Sunday Times. Is it a noospaper catch?"

"No catch at all. The News of the People explained yesterday why we are paying £5 for a chocolate box. The boxes are made by the hundred. What we want is proof when and where it was found."

"A treasure 'unt?"

"Not exactly, but something like it. How did you get this box?"

"Suppose I say my boy friend gave it me?"

"Then I must see your boy friend and find out how he got it."

"And I lose five pounds?"

"Not necessarily," said Roger patiently. "If it is what we want, you will at least share the reward."

Ada White eyed him cautiously. Then she said: "The woman I do for gave it to me. She didn't 'ad larf. She was in the Strand outside the Three Feathers—"

"Next to the Jollity Theatre?"

"That's right. She met an ole friend and asked 'im to 'ave a bit of supper somewhere and then come 'ome with her. A gent nipped out of a taxi and she nipped in and there was the chocolates. She ate the soft ones and gave the rest to me. There's four left now."

She opened the box to prove the truth of her story. Roger did not doubt it. Nor did he doubt that so far as it went, it also proved the truth of Wilfrid Mounsey's story.

"Who is the lady you work for?"

"Mrs. Rickett. Better known on the 'alls as Miss Geraldine Bulmer, but she is resting at present."

"Could you disturb her?"

"She ain't in."

"Oh, I see. She is resting professionally. When will she be in?"

"Dunno."

"Who is the gentleman friend?" Roger asked. The story would not be so good if Mrs. Rickett was a lady who made a practice of taking men home with her.

"Mr. Batten—you know, Boneless Batten the contortioner! He's all right." Ada paused a moment; she apparently read his thought. "She's all right too. No fancy work. I wouldn't be 'ere otherwise."

"I am sure you wouldn't," said Roger. "I will give you two pounds for the box. If Mrs. Rickett and Mr. Batten will call on Mr. Morant at this address and tell him just how they found it, they will get the rest of the money. That is fair, isn't it?"

"I s'pose it is," Ada said, "but what's it all about?"

"A man is accused of murder. That box may help to prove his innocence."

"Coo! But how—?"

"It is one small link that helps to prove his tale is true. You shall know all about it after Mrs. Rickett has seen Mr. Morant."

So two pound notes and the box changed owners.

"You can keep the chocolates," said Roger. "I do not think they will be necessary."

She took them, and as he returned to his Sloane Street flat he felt pleased with his success. It truly was but a small link. It did not prove Mounsey's innocence, and it certainly did not show who had shot Frederick Curtis, but it did make his story a degree less improbable.

Another surprise was in store for him. In his sitting-room Marmaduke Curtis was awaiting his return. "I hear you have been slandering me!" he shouted, jumping to his feet the moment Roger entered.

"In what way?" asked Roger coolly.

"You know in what way! And I won't have it! Unless it is stopped at once I will bring an action for damages, and let me tell you the damages will be heavy, damned heavy."

"Sit down," said Roger, "and tell me all about it."

His soothing tone did not have a soothing effect. The red of Marmaduke's face grew purple and his little eyes glittered with anger.

"I will not sit down! I hear that you are putting it about that I shot my brothers. If there could be a dam'der libel I'd like to know what it is. What d'you mean by it?"

"If you won't sit down," said Roger, "I will. Who told you this?"

"Never mind who told me," spluttered Marmaduke. "Is it true?"

"Is what true?" drawled Roger. "Do you mean is it true that you shot them? Or that I said that you shot them? You know the answer to the first better than anyone else. I can tell you the answer to the second if you will sit down and be coherent."

Marmaduke glared at him with fury. Then he plumped himself into a chair.

"Well?" he snapped.

"I am not aware that I told anyone you had shot your brothers. Acting, I hope, in the interests of justice, the question arose as to who benefited by their deaths. So far as is known you benefit more than anyone else. You inherit half Alexander's estate and you owed money to Frederick that you may not now have to repay. Is that true?"

"What have my affairs to do with you?"

"Personally, nothing. But if an innocent man is accused of murder, his friends are justified in doing all they can to detect the real criminal."

"Who is the innocent man?"

"Wilfrid Mounsey."

"Are you so sure of that?" There was a crafty look in Marmaduke's eyes. "The police do not act without good reason."

"We are wandering from the point," said Roger coldly. "You owed money to both your brothers?"

"Whether I did or not," shouted Marmaduke, "is my affair. If you dare suggest again that I had anything to do with what happened to them, I will make you pay for it."

"Yet," said Roger quietly, "you cannot explain what you were doing on the night they died."

"I was buying a car. The police know that."

"They know you say so, but they do not know where you drove it."

"Into Surrey. I told them."

"It might have been into Surrey, or it might have been to Egerton Square and Hans Avenue, or to all three. One can cover a lot of ground in a good car."

Marmaduke glared evilly at him. Much of his bluster had gone. "So that is what you have been saying?" he muttered.

"What I have been thinking," amended Roger. "To show slander or libel you must first prove publication. To whom did I say these things?"

Marmaduke looked wary. "I am warning you," he said. "You can keep your damned thoughts to yourself, but if you dare to utter them aloud it will be the worse for you. Let the police do their job and you keep clear. Otherwise you will be sorry—sorrier than you have ever been before."

With that he went. Why really had he come? Who had prompted him to do so? Those questions puzzled Roger a good deal. But before night he was to be puzzled much more, though not about Marmaduke.

XVII. AT THE PLAY

At Ashcomb Roger had promised Lotta Denys that he would see her in the play at the Cardinal Theatre as soon as he had a free evening. Frank Rudway offered him seats and said rather gloomily it would be a kindness if he spread himself as far as he could.

That night Roger tried to get into touch with Gordon Lisle to tell him the search for the chocolate box was over. For once the "biggest circulation" had not scored, but he was duly grateful for what his friend had done and knew his help might still be needed. But London has no monopoly of crime and Lisle had dashed out of town on other business.

No one pays for a seat at a theatre if he can get it for nothing. Roger sent in his card and was promptly awarded a seat in the stalls.

He entered just as the lights went down and the curtain rose. The house was not empty but it was far from full. The cheaper seats were fairly well patronised but there were many vacant stalls. It has been said that the success of a play may be judged by the number of tweed suits in the front of the house. If it is doing well there will be a smartly-dressed audience. If it is failing, seats will be given to those who do not wear orthodox attire, or whose "tails" and dinner jackets smell of moth-ball. Judged by that standard, "paper" was lavishly represented.

The first thing that intrigued Roger was that he felt sure he knew the lady next to whom he was sitting, but he could not think where he had met her. She was smartly dressed in a very low-necked frock and she seemed from the start to enjoy thoroughly all that the author offered. Lotta's appearance was the signal for a round of applause and while she was on the stage the play went with a swing. The part suited her, and "Freddie" and her other admirers played up well enough; the trouble was that the plot and the situations were so threadbare.

That did not seem to worry Roger's neighbour. The man she was with whispered to her occasionally, apparently telling her what was coming. Either he had seen the play before, or many like it.

"Don't tell me. That spoils it."

Such, more than once, was the lady's reply. Her voice was not unfamiliar, but still he could not place it. Roger found himself more interested in the identity of his neighbour than in Lotta's love affairs, though the latter with her roguish glances and quick mendacities won many laughs.

He dropped his programme to get a better look at the lady's face when he bent forward to recover it. But that was not successful. It was not until the lights went up that he knew.

His neighbour was Helen Curtis's sister, Mrs. Evelyn Parr.

He turned away and joined those who were making for the bar. In a poor light, a woman in the full war paint of her smartest evening frock may not look very much like the same woman seen only once and in her outdoor attire. But there could be no doubt of the fact.

If Evelyn Parr had accompanied Helen Curtis to that play on the second night, why should she come again a few days later? How could she revel in the stage surprises and say, "Don't tell me. That spoils it"?

In the foyer he met Rudway. "What do you think of it?" the manager asked.

"Better than I expected," said Roger. "Not such a bad house either."

"It wouldn't be, if they had paid for their tickets."

"Did the people sitting next to me pay?"

"Want to know particularly?"

"I do rather," said Roger.

Rudway slipped into the booking office and soon returned.

"Oddly enough," he said, "they did. Why do you want to know?"

"Just curiosity. Is Mr. Morant here to-night?"

"Not yet."

"I thought he always came. Has a box, I suppose?"

"First tier, nearest stage, o.p. Sure to come in before the end to take Lotta to supper."

"She is very good," Roger remarked.

"Want to see her?"

"I don't think so. If she is engaged, what about your having a bit of supper with me?"

"Don't mind if I do."

The lights were still up when Roger returned to his seat. His neighbour looked round and their glances met. She stared as if she too were conscious of a previous meeting, but could not quite recollect the occasion.

"Do you like it as much the second time?" Roger smiled.

"The second time? I haven't—" she began. Then she remembered! She flushed, but started to speak more quickly. "Every bit. I always come several times to a play I like. And Lotta Denys is wonderful, isn't she? I could come every night to see her, couldn't you?"

"Hardly that," said Roger, "but she is good. For a woman to fib so prettily when she is in a tight corner is an art in itself—don't you think so?"

Evelyn Parr did not reply, and the curtain went up. Roger doubted if she enjoyed the later acts as much as she had done the first. She talked and laughed less, and seemed preoccupied. Nor did he follow the action very closely as he too was thinking of other things.

But his attention was recaptured when "Freddie" broke his braces in trying to crawl under the bed.

"Now I am indeed undone."

He got out the brilliant line himself and it produced a laugh. Roger glanced at his watch. The time was just five minutes to ten.

He would have remained in his seat during the next interval, but Mrs. Parr and her escort went out. He followed and saw, not to his surprise, that she went to the telephone box in the foyer. He would have laid long odds that she was speaking to Helen Curtis.

When the curtain rose for the final act Mr. Morant was in his box. He looked very smart with his fresh colouring, his thick white hair, a gardenia in his buttonhole. As he glanced over the partially filled house it did not appear that the attendance disappointed him. Happy are those who can afford their hobbies!

The third act, of course, cleared up all the complications. Lotta persuaded her husband that she knew he was returning and so invited her friends to come to her room to see if he would be jealous. As he was jealous, he must love her. And as he loved her, she was the happiest woman alive and wanted nothing more!

The curtain fell to loud applause and Lotta had many recalls. Those who only paid for their entertainment with their clapping did not stint it. Half an hour later Roger and Frank Rudway had ordered their supper. Three quick Martinis dispelled something of the manager's gloom, or at least made him more talkative.

"I discovered Lotta," he said. "She is not a great actress and she never will be. She's a clever little woman up to a point, and in the right sort of play with proper support she'd go a long way. I got Mr. Morant interested in her and that spoilt her. He doesn't mind what he spends to please her, so she wants to be the whole show."

"That often happens, doesn't it?" asked Roger.

"It always happens if the woman gets her way. But it is wrong. A man who knows two tricks cannot give a conjuring entertainment; but his two tricks may be very effective if they are brought out at the right time and in the right way. It's like that with Lotta. A little of a thing may be good, but the public does not want a whole night of it."

He would have talked the whole night of Lotta. At one time, it appeared, he had wished to marry her. The wish was still there, but she was not now so keen on the idea. There were, however, other things Roger wanted to know.

"Did you alter the play much after the first night?" he asked.

"We made a few cuts and took it a bit faster."

"Does it run now as it did on the second night?"

"Pretty much. You can't keep on altering it."

"I suppose not. I had a queer fancy while it was being played. Would it have been possible for me to slip out without anyone knowing it?"

Rudway looked at him as though not quite seeing what he meant.

"You were alone, weren't you?"

"I was. But I suppose the man at the door, or the commissionaire outside would see me go?"

"Of course they would. At least they ought to."

"But if I could use the stage door?"

"Still more impossible. There is always someone there, or we should have all sorts of people pushing in."

"Then, if I bet you five pounds you couldn't get out during the show, and get back, and no one know it, I should win?"

"Is it a bet?" asked Rudway.

"No. I am only asking."

Roger refilled his guest's glass for him.

"Of course I could do it. There are some steps and a sort of chute beyond the stage door where we sometimes take in props. I could easily get out there and, if I left it unfastened, I could get back. It opens on to the same passage as the stage door. Anyone hanging about outside would see me—if there was anyone—but no one inside would know of it. I'd like to take the bet."

"You are too good," laughed Roger. "But my curiosity is satisfied. What sort of a run do you expect?"

"That depends on Mr. Morant," Rudway replied. "We are losing money already. The first-night notices were so bad. But there is always a chance things may improve if we hang on. Lotta won't let him throw it up too soon. Bad for her reputation!"

XVIII. THE OTHER MAN?

"Any news for me?" asked Inspector Goff.

"Quite a lot," Roger answered. "How can you best release Wilfrid Mounsey without damage to your reputation?"

"My reputation can take care of itself, but the best way will be to clap someone else in his place. What have you got hold of?"

It was the morning after his visit to the Cardinal Theatre. Roger felt there was a good deal he would like to discuss. He did not want any credit for himself, but he did desire to help in the disentanglement of the queer affair in which they were engaged.

"First there is this. I have traced the box of chocolates that Mounsey left in his taxi."

Goff said he had seen the advertisement and had read the appeal in the News of the People. Roger told of his call on Ada White in Lauderdale Mansions.

"We are playing fair," he added, "we are not springing this on you after your counsel has poured contempt on the chocolate box story."

"I appreciate that," said Goff, "and if the girl's mistress confirms the story, I am willing to believe that the box she found was the one Mounsey lost. But it does not help a lot, does it? It still remains that Mounsey, so far as we know, was Frederick Curtis's only visitor that night; that he suppressed all mention of his return visit; and that his prints are on the gun."

"Agreed," said Roger. "But if his story was true in one detail, it may be in all. And if we show he was the sort of fellow who would leave the chocolates for his girl in his cab, it makes other things easier to understand. But let us forget him for a moment. You remember Helen Curtis told us she went to the Cardinal Theatre that night with her sister, Mrs. Parr?"

"And Mrs. Parr confirmed it. So did Mr. Morant."

"Morant said she was there, but he did not know anything about her companion, except that it was not her husband. Mrs. Parr said she was with her sister. It is not true."

"How do you know?"

"I was at the Cardinal last night and the woman sitting next to me was Mrs. Parr. It is very unusual to go to the same show twice in ten days, especially when the tickets on the second occasion have to be paid for, but, apart from that, it was obvious from her manner she had not seen it before. When I spoke to her and asked if she liked it as much as on her previous visit, she started to say the it was the first time she had been. Then she recognised me and rather weakly said she did not mind how often she saw Lotta Denys."

"Assuming you are right," said Goff, "what do you make of it?"

"I am quite sure I am right. At the next interval Mrs. Parr went to the telephone, no doubt to let her sister know what had happened. If they both stick to their story, as they probably will, her second visit will not prove she was not there on the night of the murder, and there is only my word for the giggles and the 'Don't tell me' to her companion."

"Are you suggesting it was Mrs. Parr who shot Alexander Curtis?"

"Not for a moment. I only say we must regard Helen Curtis from a new angle."

"A liar?"

"More than that. When a woman tells her husband—I use the word for convenience—that she is going to the theatre with her sister, and it is not her sister, who is it likely to be?"

"You mean another man?"

"I do," said Roger, "and probably it had happened before. Evelyn Parr is the sort of woman who would oblige for a consideration; I should guess she is pretty hard up. Helen telephones in the morning, 'I was with you last night at a certain show,' and Evelyn says, 'Of course you were!'"

"Helen phoned her before we got to Colston Court," Goff remarked. "She told us so."

"Exactly. And later, when the matter looked serious, Evelyn asked for tickets so that she might know what the show was about, in case she was questioned."

"It is not unlikely."

"We know things were at breaking-point between Helen and Alexander, and if she was carrying on with another man the whole affair assumes a new shape. We have taken the view that she wanted Alexander to marry her, not because she loved him but because she regarded it as her right, and it would regularise her position. But would she really have wanted that if she cared for someone else?"

"What is the answer?" asked Goff.

"Helen is not a nice woman. Her early history may call for sympathy; probably it does; but she did not play the game by Alexander. She did not love him; there is no pretence of that. Why did she demand marriage? I suggest she was putting her claim as high as she could in order to get the largest possible settlement from him. If he refused, she threatened to apply on her own account for a divorce from her lunatic husband, admitting she had been living with Alexander. She could even sue Alexander for breach of promise of marriage. It would be the first case of its kind, and I do not pretend to say what her chance of success would be; but it would be mud for the highly respected family solicitor. She counted on a big cash settlement; then she could marry the other man."

"But that gives her no motive for killing Alexander," objected Goff.

"I never thought she did kill Alexander. I am wondering if Alexander knew or suspected anything about the other man, and that was why he destroyed the old will without her knowledge and, of course, without the other man's knowledge."

"Are you suggesting the other man did the killing?"

"It is not impossible," said Roger.

"His motive being to get Helen and the money it was supposed she would receive under the will?"

"I have heard of things less probable."

"There is just one point," said Goff. "Helen and Alexander were not married. Therefore, if he knew or suspected there was another man, it would not be a question of divorce. He could just tell her to clear out."

"Hence the pretence that she was with her sister."

"As Alexander was dead, why keep up the pretence?"

"If she had said she was going with a sister, she may have thought it best to stick to the story. Alexander was assumed to have committed suicide and it would not have sounded too well to say she was out with another man, especially as she was posing as the long-suffering 'wife.' We shall never know Alexander's side of the affair. He wanted to part from Helen and to marry Dreda Costello, and he wanted to arrange it all without scandal. That, I think, is undoubtable."

"It is a lot of theory to base on Evelyn Parr's 'Don't tell me,'" muttered the detective.

"I am as certain as I can be," said Roger, "that she was seeing the show for the first time. If Helen Curtis was there with another woman, why say it was her sister? I am convinced it was a man. It is a case of cherchez l'homme. Have you come across anyone who would fill the bill?"

Goff shook his head.

"We have been keeping an eye on Helen Curtis, though not for that reason. There is no man with whom she associates."

"Since the suicide idea failed," Roger remarked, "she and her man would be too wily to be seen together."

"Probably. But if all this is true, it still does not help Wilfrid Mounsey. How will you link Helen's supposed man with the death of Frederick?"

"That we have still to discover. Alexander and Fredrick were very intimate. If Alexander suspected anything, probably he told Frederick. So the only safe way was to remove them both."

"H-m-m," demurred Goff. "How was it the other brother, Marmaduke, was spared and knew nothing about it?"

"I doubt if either Alexander or Frederick trusted Marmaduke as implicitly as they trusted one another. He did get confidences from them, but I do not think they told him everything."

"Marmaduke cannot have been at the theatre," said Goff. "There is no doubt he was out in his car, though there may be doubts as to where he went."

"I am not picturing Marmaduke as Helen's boy-friend. They hate one another; there is no eyewash about that, Of course Marmaduke may be the villain—though he called last night and threatened me with an action for slander if I said so! I am wondering who put him up to that."

"Helen may have been at the theatre with a man, but it is a long jump from that to say that the man was the murderer. How can he have been, unless she was an accomplice? They returned together, he did the killing and left her to sleep there till it was discovered—is that likely?"

"No," said Roger, "it is not. I cannot see Helen doing that; I have said so from the first. Something does not quite fit. But there is another very different line that may lead somewhere."

"What is that?"

"Last week-end I was at Ashcomb, Mr. Morant's country place. He plays the local squire very handsomely, though whether he will be successful in his political ambitions remains to be seen. You will remember he told us he spent the night of the murder at his theatre, seeing how the audience reacted to the cuts and changes in the play?"

"That's right." Goff nodded.

"The leading lady, for whom he seems to have a pronounced weakness, and his manager were my fellow guests. It appears on the second night the lady said a line that really belonged to one of the other players. Not a very brilliant one; 'I am undone'—when his braces broke. She did not get it right and it upset the man who should have said it. Yet Morant knew nothing about it. Odd, wasn't it?"

Goff eyed him shrewdly. "What exactly are you getting at?"

"If Morant did not hear that—where was Morant? Another odd thing. That bit is said at five minutes to ten, and it was at five minutes to ten according to our reckoning that Frederick Curtis's second visitor was seen by Colonel Parsons to leave the house."

"You are suggesting that Morant was the second visitor?"

"I would hardly go as far as that," Roger replied. "Association with people like you makes one suspicious of everybody. If for any reason that suspicion points at Morant, the fact that he missed the side-splitting witticism misappropriated by his leading lady cracks his alibi."

"If it does—yes."

"And there is this. I ascertained from his manager, Rudway, that it would be quite possible for anyone who knew his way about at the back of the theatre to get out through a sort of goods entrance, not of course used at night, and to get back again unobserved."

Goff did not immediately reply. He opened a drawer and took out some papers.

"Can you tell me Morant's motive for the crimes?" he asked.

"Afraid I can't," Roger replied cheerily. "I could of course imagine plenty, but I haven't an atom of proof."

"You can definitely rule out Morant," said Goff. "Incredible as it may seem, we sometimes think of things all by ourselves. In case we cannot think, we have that blessed word routine to fall back on. We had no reason to suspect Morant, but it was part of the job to check his alibi. He was undoubtedly at the theatre that night. After each of the acts he visited Lotta Denys in her dressing-room. The dresser vouches for it. Between the acts he visited the box-office, and was also in the bar. After the play he spoke to Helen Curtis and took Lotta to supper. To get to Egerton Square and back would take at least an hour. Or, if he visited Hans Avenue as well, an hour and a half. I think you can take it he was never out of view for more than twenty minutes at any one time, and then he was presumably in his box."

"The fact that he missed my pet line," said Roger, "being because it was uttered while he was at the box-office or in the bar?"

"I think that is the obvious explanation," Goff nodded.

"Well, one cannot expect every brainwave to be a winner. News to date: we have got Mounsey's chocolate box and Helen Curtis did not spend the evening with her sister. As they say in the children's game, I think we are getting warmer."

XIX. THE WARNING

GORDON Lisle was back in town and that night he came round to Roger's flat. Each had news for the other.

"This is the chocolate box," said Roger, displaying his two-pound purchase. "You must let your readers know it has been recovered, though, for once in a way, not by you. But take all the credit you can."

"We never exceed the truth," Lisle assured him. "We may remind our readers of our inquiry and say what we wanted is now found. We can only hint at its great importance. It ought to help young Mounsey, but I have found something that may help more."

"What is that?"

"It is your case that more or less at the precise moment Mounsey left through the garden for the second time, someone else arrived at the front door, was admitted by Frederick Curtis, did the shooting, and was seen by Colonel Parsons when he quitted?"

"That is right."

"We have found a man who saw him arrive."

"You have!" cried Roger. "That is splendid! Who is your man? Can he describe the fellow he saw?"

"It isn't quite so splendid as that," said Lisle. "At the corner of Egerton Square, in the main road, there is a newspaper shop. It was shut, but when the old buffer to whom it belongs went out with his dog between half-past nine and ten, he saw someone in dark clothes, felt hat and mackintosh, hurrying towards No. 3."

"Did he see him go in?"

"Unfortunately he did not."

"The hat and mackintosh are useful, as Mounsey wore the like. Didn't he see his face?"

"No. He wondered which of his customers it might be, as he supplies most of the residents. But he could not identify him."

"He was not a resident, but your man cannot swear he actually entered the house?"

"No."

"Bad luck," muttered Roger, very disappointed.

"Not so bad as all that," said Lisle, who enjoyed tantalising his friend. "The dog played its part."

"What did the dog do?"

"What does a dog generally do? It reached a lamp-post. Its owner waited and looked round. The man had disappeared. There had not been time for him to reach the end of the square, there is a long blank wall before you get to the main road, so he must have gone in at one of those houses, one, three, five, seven or nine."

"He could not say which?"

"I have a sort of feeling," said Roger, "that our man would have come in a car."

"Of course he would. But you don't drive up in state to commit murder. Nor, if his car was outside, would he have left through the garden."

"That is true. He probably parked the car a street or two away."

"Undoubtedly," said Lisle. "But I have not done. My young sleuth is a lad of ideas. He promptly called on all the other houses on that side of the square and asked if there had been a visitor between 9.30 and ten on that Friday night. There had not. Therefore, the man must have gone to No. 3. Frederick Curtis admitted him, and is no longer alive to tell the tale."

"Your young sleuth deserves a rise," said Roger, "and I hope you will see he gets it. It makes my theory look pretty good. I do not doubt your newsman saw the actual murderer. What a pity he did not see a little more!"

"But it will be an awkward point for the prosecution to get over," said Lisle, "and for that we can give ourselves a pat on the back."

"With both hands," Roger agreed, "but I do not quite know how it will sound in court. Your newsman may stick to his story all right, but, to prove the caller went to No. 3, we apparently have to call the residents and the maids of all the adjoining houses to show he did not go elsewhere. Under cross-examination some of them may get into tangles. However, I have another job for the brainy lad."

"What is that?"

Roger told of his meeting with Mrs. Parr and his conviction that Helen Curtis was at the theatre on the night of the crime, not with her sister, but with a man. "Find him for us and we will be getting on!"

"But how does that help young Mounsey?" Lisle wanted to know.

"It helps the whole affair," said Roger. "You must get all the pieces before you can put the puzzle together."

"Not too easy," returned Lisle thoughtfully. "If Helen Curtis had a boy friend unknown to her so-called husband, she would take care to keep it as secret as possible. If we could burgle her flat to find her love-letters it might help, but we draw the line at that."

"Do you?" said Roger. "How extraordinarily conscientious! Of course Scotland Yard has search warrants for the asking, and Alexander's effects have been duly examined. Helen may have taken her own precautions."

Lisle lit himself another cigarette. Then he said: "I would give a good deal to know whether it is one murderer we are looking for, or two!"

"It would be useful."

"Alexander's case seems comparatively simple. It might be suicide, though we agree that can almost be ruled out. It might be murder by brother Marmaduke. He knew there was no will, and he also knew the complicated state of affairs between Alexander and Helen should direct suspicion away from himself. Or it might be murder by Helen after she got home from the theatre."

"How about the supposed boy friend?"

"If he was with her at the theatre, as you say, he cannot have been killing Alexander. Of course he could have gone back with her and they could have done it together; but that means he went off and left her alone with the body until such time as someone found it in the morning. Is she hard-boiled enough for that?"

"I doubt it," said Roger. "I told Goff so."

"I doubt it too," said Lisle.

"Yet you said it was simple!"

"I said it was comparatively simple. By that, I meant compared with Frederick's case. Helen, Helen and her lover, or Marmaduke might have killed Alexander; but who killed Frederick? I admit you can make some sort of a case against Marmaduke, but not a strong one. He would know that his brother was left-handed, but is the motive sufficient? Some debts that might possibly be wiped out and the care of Delia and her fortune for a year. Why kill Frederick for such shadowy gains when killing Alexander makes him rich? He would be eliminating someone who might suspect him—but why should Frederick suspect him? We have no real reason for supposing that."

"Go on," said Roger. "It is useful to have one's own ideas expressed from a different angle."

"So if we acquit Marmaduke, and obviously Helen and her unknown friend had nothing against Frederick, we find the suspects for the Alexander case are not suspects for the brother's case. Yet we proceed on the supposition that the same hand was guilty of both crimes!"

"What is your summary in Frederick's case?" asked Roger.

"First, suicide, which we ruled out. Secondly, Wilfrid Mounsey, who has undoubtedly got himself in a tight corner. Third, the unknown visitor seen by the newsagent, who might have been Marmaduke had the motive been more convincing."

"Marmaduke being the only common factor," Roger remarked. "Yes, but if one hand was guilty of both crimes, there is still something that puzzles me."

"What is that?"

"The mentality of the murderer," said the crime editor. "Would anyone kill two men in such precisely similar circumstances, with the same sort of trick to establish the time, at the same minute in each case, and hope to get away with supposed suicides?"

"Certainly not," said Roger "That is why he did it!"

"Too subtle for me," said Lisle.

"I don't think so. Our criminal, for reasons as yet unknown, decided to kill two brothers on the same night. That was going to look odd in any event. Would it have looked any less odd if one death had been at nine o'clock and the other at ten? He did not expect his clock and watch tricks to be discovered. If murder was not suspected, the identity of time would in itself suggest some sort of suicide pact. If for any reason murder was suspected, the hour was fixed to suit the alibi."

"You may be right," Lisle agreed. "On the whole I do not see how our criminal could have done much better in the time at his disposal. But who the devil is he?"

At that moment the telephone bell rang. Roger picked up the receiver.

"Is that Mr. Roger Bennion?" asked a muffled voice.

"It is. Who are you?"

"Never mind me. You are interested in the Curtis suicide cases?"

"I am."

"Then take the advice of a friend," said the voice, "and lay off. Mind your own business and let the police mind theirs. Understand?"

"Who are you?"

"A friend who doesn't want you to play the principal part at a funeral. This is serious. Drop the whole thing or your suicide will be the next. You won't get another warning."

"Hullo . . . hullo..."

The voice ceased. Roger tapped the instrument and got the attention of the operator.

"Can you tell me where that call came from?" he asked.

"From a call office in Sloane Square," was the reply.

"Then you cannot tell me who it was, or reconnect me?"

"Afraid not."

"What was it?" asked Lisle, as Roger replaced the receiver.

"Someone with a taste for melodrama. Unless I drop the Curtis cases my suicide is the next on the list. My last warning."

"Will you act on the advice?" his friend inquired.

"Need you ask? Either it is the act of a silly fool and means nothing, or else someone is getting the wind up and it means a lot. When we know who it was your newsvendor saw, and who really went with Helen Curtis to the theatre, it will not be long before we understand the whole affair."

XX. THE CHOCOLATES AGAIN

It was not until the next afternoon that Roger was able to see Margot. Ascertaining that she had come to town he hurried round to the flat and was received in the same room as before. He thought he had given her good news and hoped his further tidings would be still more encouraging. He was distressed to find her almost more upset and unhappy than before.

"Have you heard?" she asked, directly he was shown in. "The trial begins next week."

"I had not heard that," Roger said. "I hope it means Wilfrid will be free all the sooner."

"I don't see how it can. Uncle Victor says it is no good putting that woman who had the chocolates into the witness-box. He tells me to be brave, but I can see he doesn't think we have a chance."

She burst into tears.

For a moment Roger did not know what to say. He could understand that in her overwrought condition she was suffering even more than the man who was in prison. Probably every set-back seemed unduly terrible.

Her predicament was a continual agony.

"Things cannot be so bad as that," he said gently. "Have you told your uncle about Wilfrid Mounsey and yourself?"

"No," she sobbed. "I haven't told anyone but you."

His first thought was that she might have confided in Mr. Morant and had found him more blameful than sympathetic. Now he saw it was the lack of a confidante that made her so intensely unhappy.

"I have heard something that may help quite a lot," he said. "It is going to be all right. So no more tears. Tell me first why he does not propose to call Mrs. Rickett."

Margot dried her eyes and soon recovered something of her normal manner.

"Sorry I was such a fool," she muttered. "I was feeling so miserable, I believe I should have broken down whoever spoke to me. I am better now."

"Of course you are. Did Mr. Morant see Mrs. Rickett?"

"She went to his office, but he says she would be such a bad witness he would be afraid to call her."

"What is wrong with her?"

"I don't know exactly. He thinks the jury would not believe her, and a discredited witness is worse than no witness at all."

"That is sometimes true," Roger admitted, "but I hardly see how it applies here. I must see her myself, and I will also see him."

"What is the other news?" asked Margot.

Roger told her of the newsvendor's story as unearthed by Gordon Lisle's bright young man. It cheered her a lot.

"That is splendid," she said. "If only we could find out who it was! It fits in and makes Wilfrid's story true! May I tell Uncle Victor?"

"Of course. I was meaning to see him myself to ask when I might bring the man along. I did not realise that time was so short."

"I expect he will be in soon. Won't you wait and see him? Have some tea or something."

Roger had already had tea, but he decided to wait for Mr. Morant. If the hours were so few, each one was important.

"Probably matters will not go very far next week," he said. "In fact I am rather surprised the case is being taken at all."

"Why?"

"Because no one would charge Wilfrid with killing Alexander Curtis, and to push on with the case respecting

Frederick would mean that the police have definitely decided that the two crimes are distinct and separate. I doubt if they are prepared to do that just yet."

He thought it better not to tell her of his talk with Goff and of the inspector's readiness to accept the chocolate story. Nor did he mention his own theory as to Helen Curtis's gentleman friend. He wanted to cheer her as much as he could, but he hoped to get things a good deal more clear before he talked about them. And there was no point in mentioning the threat to himself of the night before.

"Then what will happen next week?" Margot was asking.

"Probably nothing. An adjournment."

"That means he will still be kept in prison?"

"I am afraid so. They do not allow bail in these cases."

"I am to see him to-morrow," she said.

"You will not tell him—?"

"No! I wouldn't be such a selfish little beast when he is in such trouble. I shall let him know you are helping us and it will be all right. I shall tell him about the chocolates, whatever Uncle Victor says. And about the newspaper man too. I won't let him think there is a single doubt anywhere."

She was plucky. Roger knew she would play her part, whatever her secret dreads might be. Then she heard her uncle return and in a few moments he was with them. He greeted Roger cordially.

"Margot tells me you are not calling Mrs. Rickett as a witness?" Roger remarked.

"I am in doubt about it," said Mr. Morant. "Have you seen her?"

"No. I saw the maid, Ada White. The story sounded true to me."

"Mrs. Rickett is a very flashy type of person. She is known on the music-halls as Geraldine Bulmer, and like many of her class she sees in a case of this sort a chance to advertise herself. Sir John Gore will prosecute. She will try to be smart when he cross-examines her and that will be fatal."

"How do you mean?"

"I asked her how she came to take the chocolates that were not hers. She said she thought she had as much right to them as anyone else. I enquired if she had seen the advertisement of the reward. She said no; she would have found half a dozen boxes for that! Sir John will lead her gently on, and will have little difficulty in persuading the jury the whole story is a put-up job to help the accused. If she is our chief witness, heaven help us!"

"But the story does not depend on her," said Roger. "Her companion, Boneless Batten, will confirm it and so will Ada White. Also it was not a question of producing any box of chocolates; it had to be a particular make, put up in a particular way."

"If it were true," said Morant, "it would only show Wilfrid Mounsey had such a box of chocolates. It would be no evidence as to what he did while he was in the house. If her story is not believed, it makes things all the worse. Of course the decision does not rest with me. Our counsel, Sir Norman French, will decide whether or not she shall be called. I know how anxious Margot is, so I felt bound to tell her of the difficulties."

"But Mr. Bennion has discovered something else," said the girl.

"What is that?" inquired the solicitor.

Roger repeated the story as told him by Gordon Lisle. Had there been no visitors at Nos. 1, 5, 7, 9 and 11 Egerton Square at the time in question, the man seen by the newsagent must have called at No. 3.

"I went to his shop to-day," he added. "His name is George Penniquick. You will find him an admirable witness in every way. Slow, but sure of his facts. I can arrange for you to see him."

"I certainly will," said Mr. Morant. "This sounds important. Your theory is that Frederick Curtis himself admitted this visitor directly he rang or knocked?"

"And he did the shooting!" cried Margot. "Then he went out through the garden and Colonel Parsons saw him!"

"It certainly seems possible. I do not know that we need call all the neighbours. An affidavit from each of them, if we can get it, may do. It really turns on Penniquick's story. Whether the man could have reached the end of the road before he turned round; or whether he might have crossed to the other side, Frederick Curtis would have had to let him in almost immediately, or he would have been seen on the doorstep."

"Probably the man had telephoned Frederick Curtis," said Roger, "to make sure he would be in. He must have been some one Curtis knew well and whom he would probably admit at once."

"Who was the man?" asked Margot.

"A natural question, my dear," said her uncle, "but one that we happily do not have to answer. If we can show beyond doubt there was such a man it will serve our purpose. Meanwhile, I would ask Mr. Bennion to keep it all under his hat. Don't let Inspector Goff or anyone else know about it, and don't tell him of the lady and the chocolates. The less they know of our plans, and the more surprises we can give them, the better for us."

Roger did not say how much he had already told Goff. In an ordinary way he would have taken Morant's view of the case, but if the best defence for Mounsey was to show that one person was responsible for both crimes, it might be better policy to work with the police, not against them.

"How is the play going?" he asked before he left.

"Not too well," shrugged Morant. "It may pick up. I'll give it a month anyhow. What did you think of it? Rudway told me you had been."

"It is always difficult to say why one play succeeds and another fails," Roger replied, avoiding a direct answer. "I thought Lotta Denys as charming as ever. The same, in a sense, applied to her part."

"You mean it lacks originality?"

"Some people say there are no new plots; the Greeks used them all. But certain authors have the gift of making them look new. I hope Lotta will yet pull it through. But there is one thing I would like to ask."

"Yes?"

"On the night of the crime Helen Curtis was at the play, and you told us she was not alone. Was her companion a man or a woman?"

"I think I told you her husband was not with her, but I am not sure who was. From my box I saw her in the stalls and I do not think there was an empty seat in that row, so she cannot have come alone. To the best of my belief there was a man on one side of her and a woman the other. I was too much occupied to think much about her."

"You would have recognised her sister, Mrs. Parr?"

"I do not think I should. I have only met Mrs. Parr once and that was years ago. Why are you asking?"

"Only a general check up on the stories we hear," said Roger.

When he left, Margot went with him to the door.

"Thank you for everything," she whispered. "I feel a lot better. It was my lucky day when I came to you."

"Make it Wilfrid's lucky day to-morrow," Roger laughed. "Cheer him up."

"You bet I will."

"Lauderdale Mansions," said Roger, hailing the nearest taxi. He was puzzled by Mr. Morant's attitude to Mrs. Rickett and decided to see her himself without further delay. The truth of Wilfrid Mounsey's chocolate box story did not prove a lot, but it supported the whole line of defence, and it was a picturesque detail that a jury would not forget. Surely it would be a mistake not to make the most of it.

When, however, Roger met the lady he was bound to admit there was some justification for the line the solicitor had taken.

Ada White admitted him and showed him into a small room, the walls of which were covered with photographs of actors and actresses, mostly inscribed with affectionate greetings. One frame held eight photographs of the same woman in different poses, and in costumes varying from a minimum in knickers and brassiere to elaborate evening toilets. There was no name, but he guessed it must be the woman he had come to see—Geraldine Bulmer, or in private life Mrs. Rickett.

He was studying them when the door opened and the original came in.

She was a remarkable woman. Fair, with bleached hair and blue eyes, she had the largest mouth he had ever seen. Her teeth luckily were good. She proved to have a loud voice, with an enormous laugh, and she spoke very quickly. Her face was big and she had no eyebrows at all. She was of middle height, and her age might have been anything in the early thirties.

"So it is Mr. Bunnion," she said.

"Bennion," he corrected.

"I like Bunnion better. What have you come about?"

"I believe you found the box of chocolates in the taxi that I advertised for?"

"I did. What's the game, Mr. Bunnion?"

"Bennion," he murmured gently.

"I prefer Bunnion. Reminds me of Pilgrim's Progress. And the grimmest pill is when there is no progress. Then you get the boot. And it is only the barefooted who know where the shoe pinches."

She rattled this off very quickly and opened her cavern of a mouth to let forth a mighty laugh.

"Suppose you've never seen my act?" she added.

"I do not think I have."

"You've missed a treat. Jim and Gerry. Cross-talk comedians. Jim wrote most of the patter. Sometimes handed it me straight off the ice as we went along. That took keeping up with. Sharp as a needle and quick as lightning was Jim."

"Are you not still partners?" asked Roger politely.

"He's in hospital so I'm resting till he's better. No one like Jim for getting the laughs. It's easy once you get 'em going, but it's starting 'em that is the trouble. Soon as the giggling begins you're all right. Quick fire, that's the secret."

"So that they do not have time to think they've heard it before?"

"That's a nasty one." She bellowed a big laugh. "The oldest joke is new to someone."

"Yes. But—"

"I know; you're here on business. Wasn't I promised three quid when I called on Less-Uncle?"

"Less-Uncle?"

"Morant, if you prefer it. I get a lot of fun out of names. Well, wasn't I?"

"Do you mean Mr. Morant did not give you the money?"

"He certainly did not. Said he must think it over. He would produce the dibs if he wanted me again. How's that for obtaining goods under false pretences?"

Roger produced his pocket book and took out three pound notes.

"I put in the advertisement," he said, "and I will pay if you will tell me the story."

"That's fair. But Ida told you the story, didn't she? Ida!" She shouted the name in a voice that could probably be heard in every flat in the building. Ada White appeared so quickly that she must have been listening at the door.

"Ida, what did you tell this gentleman about the box of chocolates I brought home?"

"I said as 'ow you found 'em in a taxi-cab outside the Jollity Theatre that Friday night."

"That's right," said Mrs. Rickett. "So I did. What more do you want to know?"

"Who was with you?" asked Roger.

"Leo. Boneless Batten. Ever heard of him?"

"Afraid not. What is his address?"

"Now you're asking. He's not the sort that has an address. But I can tell you his agent. Write Bill Batten, care of Schenks, 3001 Shaftesbury Avenue."

"Bill Batten—I thought you said Leo?" Again the big laugh.

"Boneless Batten – Boney—Napoleon – Leo. All his chums call him Leo."

"He will confirm the story?"

"Course he will. He ate some of the chocs."

"What time was it?"

"A bit before eleven. We had some supper at Frastino's, then he brought me home and came in for a last one. I told all that to Less-Uncle."

"You are prepared to swear to it in court?"

"Why not?" she grinned. "You would be amazed at my swearing when I feel like it!"

Roger handed over the notes. On the whole he thought the investment a good one.

"Ta. I won't say it isn't useful while Jim is laid up. Real luck, and you're a real gent."

As she spoke, she opened a bag to put away the money. She, of course, looked at herself in her mirror.

"Holy smoke! I've forgotten my eyebrows!"

She seized a pencil and quickly added dark lines where her brows had been; her mouth open like a letter box all the time. The lines were much darker than her hair and the effect was, at any rate, striking.

"That better?" she asked.

"Undoubtedly," said Roger.

"Fancy me forgetting 'em! If you was Jim you would say it was because ours wasn't an 'igh-brow show." She gave another big laugh. Then she said: "Now, Barney, you tell me something."

"Barney?"

"Bunnion—Corns – Wheat – Barney. That's how I get my names. Quick thinking. What did old Less-Uncle mean by wanting to know if I was a respectable married woman? What business is it of his? I told him, whether I was or not, he needn't have any hopes. I found the chocolates, whatever I was, without his insinuendoes, as Jim calls 'em."

"It is like this, Mrs. Rickett—" Roger began.

"Call me Gerry—even if it makes you think of something else!"

"If you are put in the witness-box, Mr. Morant wants your story to be believed. He wants to show you are a simple straightforward witness. He is a little afraid of your sense of humour. We should ask for a plain statement of what happened. If you thought of any wise-cracks or fancy names they would not help us."

"A laugh does everyone good."

"Not in court," said Roger, "unless the judge makes the joke."

"But look here: what is the case all about? If it was murder, who was done in?"

"Was the choc'lates poisoned?" asked Ada, who had lingered by the door, in sudden fear. "I 'ad the last this mornin'!"

"That was the poisoned one," said her mistress. "You buzz off, Ida, and get yourself a big glass of soap and water and drink it quick!"

"They were not poisoned," said Roger. "A man who is accused of murder accounts for his time by saying he went back to a certain house for a box of chocolates he had left behind. His story is doubted, partly because he had no chocolates. He accounts for that by saying he left them in a taxi. If we can show that is true it might help quite a lot."

"Forgetful devil, ain't he?" said Gerry. "But it's true enough. I don't say I could swear to the bloke what got out of the cab, but I can swear to the chocs! So can Leo and Ida. But say—"

"What is it?" asked Roger, as she paused.

"Whose side exactly is Less-Uncle on?"

"On ours. He is the solicitor for the defence."

"Then why did he want to choke me off with his respectability? I'll bet I am a dam' sight more respectable than he is, if the truth's known. Who but me can prove the chocs was there? And if he wants to prove it, why is he so sniffy about me being a witness? If I do sometimes open my mouth and put my foot in it—Jim always says there is plenty of room!—it is the truth that matters, isn't it?"

"It is," said Roger. "And I have no doubt we shall want you to tell it."

XXI. THE AFFAIR IN THE STREET

As Roger returned to Sloane Street he wondered if he was making too much of the chocolate box incident. On the whole he did not think he was. He must insist on Morant calling Gerry as a witness. She might earn a stiff reproof from the judge if her style was too unorthodox, but she would probably impress a jury quite favourably. The point that she could establish was of minor importance, but he had known so many cases where much had turned on what seemed to be a trifle. When different people swear to different stories, and where the evidence is mainly circumstantial, one small piece of fact may weigh heavily and even turn the scale.

On reaching his flat his man, Froy, told him that Miss Dreda Costello had been ringing him up.

"She has something important to tell you, sir, and wants to know if you can go round to her studio at ten this evening."

"Of course I can," said Roger. "Get her for me."

"No good, sir. She was going out, but would be back by ten. If you did not come, she would know it was inconvenient and would ring up again in the morning."

"I will be there. What time was it when she got through?"

"Half an hour ago, sir."

While he was with Gerry Bulmer. He wondered what Dreda had to tell him. There was plenty he wanted to know, but she was concerned with Helen Curtis and Alexander. At that moment, with the trial commencing so soon, it was the defence of Wilfrid Mounsey on the charge of killing Frederick that was the more urgent.

He arranged his arrival at the studio punctually for ten o'clock. The little cul-de-sac was very dark; a detail that escaped him at first, as the headlights of his car lit up the street.

Dreda's door was closed, as it naturally would be at that time of night. He drove to the edge of the left-hand pavement, then switching off the main lights, he got out.

As he put his foot to the ground, he was conscious of two forms that came to life from an adjacent recessed doorway.

They rushed at him, and one of them aimed a blow at his head with a heavy bludgeon.

Startling and unexpected as the attack was, Roger had time to throw himself forward so that the blow missed its mark and he and his assailant rolled over together.

Then the second of the two struck at him. But in the dim light, and struggling as he was, only his shoulder was hit. In an instant he was on his feet.

Another savage blow aimed at his head was warded off by his arm, which dropped nerveless to his side. But his other arm was still useful! He struck his attacker hard and true between the eyes. The man was staggered, but he did not fall.

"Out him!"

The cry was to his companion who had scrambled up from the pavement. He rushed forward, swinging his weapon with a ferocity that was meant to kill.

Roger slipped aside.

The two were coming at him together when Dreda's door opened and a sudden flood of light illumined the scene.

Immediately both the attackers fled and Dreda herself stood in the doorway.

"What is it?" she said. "What has happened?"

"Those two men seem to have heard of your invitation," Roger answered grimly. "They had extinguished the street lights and rushed at me just as I got out of the car."

"Are you hurt?"

"My arm doesn't feel too good, but I don't think any bones are broken. They were using life-preservers or something of the sort."

"But who were they? Why did they do it? Come in and let me see if you are all right."

"If I had turned the car before I got out," he muttered, peering up the darkened street, "I would have gone after them. Not much good now."

"Never mind them. Let me see your arm."

He followed her up the stairs to her studio. She helped him take off his coat and roll up his shirt-sleeve. His arm was painful and had a nasty bruise, but he was right in saying the bone was not broken. Dreda applied some lotion and deftly rolled a bandage. There was a bruise on his shoulder but he did not worry her about that.

"Lucky you opened the door for me just when you did," he said. "If one of their blows had got home I should have gone down and they could have finished things at their leisure."

"Don't!" she shuddered. "But I didn't open the door for you. I was going out. I often do for half an hour or so last thing."

"But you 'phoned for me to call at ten o'clock."

She looked puzzled. "Afraid I did not," she said.

"My man got a message asking me to call here at ten. Your name was given, and I was told not to come earlier, or ring up, as you would be out."

"I have been in all the evening."

"Becomes more interesting, doesn't it?" Roger commented. "I arrive punctually at ten and two men have a good go at knocking me out."

"There have been one or two cases of people being robbed on dark nights," said Dreda.

"Dangerous for you."

"Artists have nothing worth stealing!"

"Yet these men were waiting in your cul-de-sac with the lights off. I have run into a lot of coincidences lately, but this looks too much according to plan. The bogus message and the waiting foot-pads. I ought perhaps to tell myself I had been warned."

"What do you mean?"

"Brother Marmaduke told me what would happen if I continued to slander him. A mysterious voice over the telephone advised me to leave the police to do their job in the Curtis cases without my interference or it would be the worse for me. Now this."

"You think Marmaduke is behind it all?"

"I have been warned not to slander Marmaduke," he smiled.

"But what will you do? It is all very well to laugh at threats, but a deliberate attempt at murder is another matter!"

Dreda's calm outlook on life was undoubtedly shaken by what had happened at her very threshold. But Roger did not want her to be unduly alarmed.

"I shall take care in future not to keep appointments on dark nights without verifying them," he said. "But it does look as though our unknown friend was getting the wind up, doesn't it?"

"Who can it be?" she asked.

"It must be someone who knew that I had met you and that a message from you would bring me along."

"Was it a woman's voice?"

"I think Froy would have smelt something wrong had it not been."

"But what woman could know—except Helen?"

Roger did not answer that.

"When I got what I thought was your message," he said, "I was rather glad, as I wanted to talk to you about Helen."

"About Helen?" she echoed.

"Yes. I suppose she has not been to see you again?"

"I am happy to say she has not."

"The thing is this. Is there any reason for believing that, although she demanded that Alexander should marry her, she really cared for someone else?"

"I do not know. Why do you ask?"

He told her of his meeting with Helen's sister at the theatre and the conclusion he had drawn from it.

"Did Alexander ever hint that he suspected there was another man?"

Dreda considered the question for some moments before she replied, her brow puckered in thought.

"We really discussed Helen very little," she said. "Alexander was essentially loyal. Had he been full of abuse for the other woman, as men sometimes are, I should have thought less of him. It was understood between us that he would get things cleared up as quickly as he could. I never bothered him if he did not want to talk about it. But once he did say that Helen must have a cunning person to advise her."

"A solicitor?"

"I don't know. Being a solicitor himself, Alexander meant to fix everything and to fix it fairly. But it seemed there was someone who always prompted Helen to ask for more."

"Probably the man I want," said Roger. "Would he be a business adviser or a lover?"

Dreda shook her head. "No use my guessing, is it?"

"No; but does it seem to you unlikely that she had some secret affair of the sort?"

"I do not want to be uncharitable, but I should think it extremely likely. She is that kind of woman. Yet I do not see how it explains Alexander's death. I told you I believed Helen was innocent of that."

Roger did not immediately reply. And she went on: "How about the poor boy who is accused of killing Frederick? Will you be able to help him?"

Before he could answer, the telephone bell rang. Dreda lifted the receiver.

"For you," she said. "Be careful!"

"Is that you, Mr. Bennion? I rang up your flat, and they gave me your number."

"Who is speaking?"

"Margot Watney. It is terribly important. I want to see you to-night. When will you be back? May I come round?"

He did not doubt it was Margot. He could recognise the voice, in spite of a certain tenseness suggestive of excitement or agitation.

"I am at Miss Costello's studio," be said. "I may be here for some little while. Will it not be better if I see you in the morning?"

"I must—I must see you to-night. Ask Miss Costello if I may come. It might be necessary to have two witnesses for what I have to say."

"Hold on a minute."

He put his hand over the mouthpiece and told Dreda what he had heard.

"You are sure it isn't another trap?" she asked.

"Our friends would hardly try the same dodge twice in one night. It is Margot all right. She wants to come here. But I think the strain is getting too much for her and she is heading for a breakdown."

"You mean we should go to her?"

"Would you?"

"If she would like me to. It must be terrible for her, with her fiancé where he is."

It was more terrible than Dreda knew. Roger again had the feeling that her calm womanly sympathy was what Margot needed.

"You there, Margot? If you really wish it Miss Costello says she will come round to you with me right away."

"Oh, thank you, thank you!"

"Is your uncle in?"

"No. He is at the theatre and will be going to supper after. He won't be back for ages."

XXII. MARGOT'S CONFESSION

There was no one about when Dreda got into Roger's car. The street lights were still out and after the brightness of her room the cul-de-sac seemed very dark indeed.

"Will you tell the police what happened?" she asked, as they moved away.

"I fear it will do no good. I couldn't give a description of the men, and would not be able to identify either of them if they were caught."

"It ought to be reported. It is not a nice thing to happen."

"Then to-morrow they shall know all about it."

"To-morrow? What about the street lights?"

"Do you mind if we go to Margot first? On the way back I will tell my tale."

He had the feeling that Margot wanted him urgently, and when he and his companion arrived at the flat he was astonished at the change in her appearance. When he left her in the afternoon she had seemed cheerful and full of hope. Now her manner was entirely different. It was difficult to describe. Not so much despair as desperation possessed her. Yet she was almost stonily calm.

He introduced the woman who had lost at the hand of a murderer the man she loved and hoped to marry, to the girl whose lover was in prison on the charge of murder—not of that man but of his brother.

Then he waited.

"I shot Frederick Curtis."

Margot said the words in a dull monotone, almost as if she did not realise their terrible meaning. Her listeners were too astonished to reply.

"I shot Frederick Curtis. He prevented Wilfrid marrying me and Wilfrid had to marry me. I never thought I should be suspected, and I wasn't. But they have accused Wilfrid, so I must tell the truth. I left the others at the theatre and went to his house and did it. If you will write it down I will sign it and you can take it to the police."

She stopped, and for many moments no one spoke. Then she asked: "Or must I write it myself?"

To that question there was no reply. Roger put another. "Have you told this to your uncle?"

"No. I do not want to see him. I would rather go to the police."

"When you do that," Roger said, "there is a lot more they will want to know."

"What?"

"You were at the theatre. Did the rest of the party know that you left them?"

"It is a two-act play at the Jollity. I sat through the first act and then slipped out as the second act started. I was at the end of the row next to Delia. She knew I went. I told her I had a headache. I was back before it finished; I do not think the others knew."

"Who were the others?"

"Rhoda and Jimmie Durrant."

"What were you wearing?"

"A black dinner frock. Outside the theatre I got a cab and came here. I put on a mackintosh and an old felt hat. I got another cab to put me down at the nearest point to Egerton Square. I suppose the newsagent and Colonel Parsons both took me for a man."

Roger was putting his questions very quietly, and she was replying in the same lifeless tone as before.

"Did Mr. Frederick Curtis admit you?"

"He did."

"What did he say?"

"He was surprised to see me, as he thought I was at the theatre. I said there was something I wanted to ask him. He took me to his room. We talked. He told me that on no account whatever would he consent to Wilfrid's marriage before he was through his exams. I shot him and I escaped through the garden. I turned on the wireless first, as I thought if anyone heard anything they might put it down to that."

"Where did you get your pistol?"

"I bought it a year ago in France. I came here for it."

"Show me exactly how you shot him."

"Why should I do that? Is it not enough that I admit it?"

"If you want the police to believe you," Roger said, "you will have to tell them everything. Suppose I am Mr. Curtis and my pipe is the pistol. Show me just how you did it."

She had been sitting almost woodenly in her chair, her eyes fixed on the ground, her body motionless. At first she seemed unable or unwilling to move. Roger offered the pipe and waited for her to take it. Dreda sat by them, equally motionless, listening to all they said.

With an effort Margot got to her feet and took the pipe in her hand. She stood by Roger's side.

"I was close to him. I shut my eyes and pulled the trigger. It made less noise than I expected. I opened my eyes and he rolled slowly on to the floor. He was dead."

"Then," said Roger, "you wiped the pistol, didn't you? And. you pressed his fingers on it. How did you do that?"

She wiped the imaginary weapon with her handkerchief, and still holding it in the handkerchief, she took Roger's right hand in her own cold hand and pressed his fingers round the bowl.

"Then I put it on the floor by his side."

"Anything else?"

"The watch. I hit the glass with the end of the pistol and broke it. Then I altered the time to nearly eleven o'clock. That that was all."

"You left through the garden. How did you get back to the theatre?"

"In another cab."

She put his pipe on the table at her side and sat down again in her chair. But Roger had not quite finished. "What time was it then?"

"I think it was a quarter to eleven. I got back to my seat before the play ended."

"A wet night, wasn't it? What did you do with the mackintosh and the hat?"

"I—I left them in the cab. The man drove away with them."

Again for several moments there was silence. A little clock on the mantelpiece ticked loudly. That was the only sound. "Will you—will you write it down? I will sign it and Miss Costello can be a witness."

"There is something you have not told me," Roger said very quietly.

"What is that?"

"You have not told me why you have made this confession."

"I did tell you. I knew I was not suspected, but I could not let them think Wilfrid did it. The only way was to tell the truth."

"The truth! What you have told us has not a word of truth in it! What is the real reason for it, Margot? I know you want to help Wilfrid, but this will not help him. The police would not be deceived for a moment."

"But it is true!" she cried, and there was a new and wilder note in her voice. "It is true. Why should they not believe it?"

"I will tell you a few reasons. In the first place I doubt if your friends at the theatre would support your story. Delia might, if you asked her. Perhaps you have already asked her. But I doubt if she would when she knew what it meant. As there was a man in the party, I do not believe you and Delia had the outside seats and he was by his sister. But that is a very minor point. Also the way you say you approached the house is the opposite way to that described by the newsagent. That does not make it impossible. What really gives you away is that Mr. Frederick Curtis being left handed was shot on the other side of the head, by someone who knew the fact. And his left hand, not his right, was pressed on to the weapon. The watch, incidentally, was put on before the glass was smashed, not afterwards. Tiny splinters showed that. But it is the reason that baffles me. Why, Margot, did you want me to take a story like that to the police?"

The, girl stared at him with fear-strained eyes. Her hands were clenched, her whole body tense. Then she seemed suddenly to collapse and she burst into tears.

"There is so little time," she sobbed. "Don't you see? I would be all right, and then they would discover the truth."

Dreda had gone to her side and put her arms round her. There was something wonderfully effective in her quiet, assured sympathy.

"Suppose I leave you two together for a few minutes," said Roger. "I will be in the next room."

There was no reply, and he did as he suggested. The adjacent room was apparently Mr. Morant's study. Feeling something of an intruder, Roger sat down and waited. Many thoughts were in his mind, but just then the uppermost was that it would be extremely awkward if the owner of the room returned and found him there. How could he account for his second visit without implicating Margot? How would she explain it?

Another thought was of thankfulness to Dreda for coming with him. It would indeed have been awkward if Margot had told her story and had then crumpled up in that way with only himself to help her. It was lucky he had thought of bringing Dreda; it was good of her to have come. What would Margot have to say when she returned to a more normal frame of mind?

That he was not to know. The minutes passed. He was almost through his second cigarette when Dreda appeared.

"She is all right," she said. "She has gone to bed and I am coming round to-morrow. We had better go."

They let themselves out of the flat and went for some way in silence. Roger was, of course, taking her back to the studio.

"She has told me everything," said Dreda, as they neared the King's Road. "She has had a ghastly time."

"When I left her this afternoon," replied Roger, "she seemed reasonably happy and was meaning to cheer up Wilfrid Mounsey when she visited him to-morrow. I cannot understand what brought about the sudden collapse and led her to tell us that fantastic story."

"It was, in a way, a tribute to you."

"You mean she was trying it on me to see if it seemed convincing?"

"Not exactly that. After you left them this afternoon her uncle told her the position was extremely difficult. He would do all that was possible, but she must be brave in case they were attempting the impossible. I gather she flared up at that and asked if he had any doubts as to Wilfrid's innocence. He replied with lawyer's jargon that everyone was innocent until he was proved to be otherwise. He was doing his best, but it would be cruel to pretend the police had not a very strong case."

"That scared her?"

"Indeed it did. She is perfectly sure that Wilfrid is not guilty, but when Mr. Morant left her she went over everything and frightened herself into believing that the only way to save him was to gain time. She believes you will discover the truth, but the trial is next week and it will be no good if the truth is not found soon enough. So she decided to confess that she had done it. She thought she could tell a convincing story and Wilfrid would be released."

"Not much gain in that," said Roger grimly, "if she was believed."

"More gain perhaps than you think," Dreda replied quietly. "Do you not see her idea?"

"Afraid I don't."

"Nothing much would be done to a young woman in her condition."

"In her condition—I see."

"She thinks she might be imprisoned, but sooner or later you would discover the truth. Then everything would be vindicated."

"My God!" said Roger. "What a wonderful thing is a woman in love!"

"That is true. Many would blame her for what has happened, but there is a streak of sheer heroism in her."

"I am glad you will be her friend."

Nothing more was said until they reached the studio. The lights in the little street were burning properly. Evidently someone had reported the state of affairs, or the policeman on his beat had discovered it. It was not necessary for them to do anything about it.

"Good-night," said Dreda. "Her faith in you is wonderful. I know you will not fail her. But you must take care of yourself."

"I shall be all right," Roger replied. "But such faith is rather frightening."

XXIII. LISLE'S BIG THOUGHT

ROGER was very busy for the next few days, but try as he might, he could get no fresh light on his problems. He received no more mysterious telephone calls, and there were no further attacks on himself. He took reasonable precautions, but nothing out of the ordinary came his way. No motor cars made sudden efforts to run him down; no hods of bricks dropped near him as he passed new buildings!

Through the agents mentioned by Gerry Bulmer he got into touch with Boneless Batten, a rather lugubrious individual—as one well might be who earned his living by twisting his body into knots that defied all the laws of anatomy.

Although annoyed by the way her uncle had frightened Margot, Roger took "Boneless" to see Mr. Morant and pointed out that if Miss Gerry was not herself an ideal witness her testimony, supported by that of her friend, could hardly be doubted.

"We will try it," the solicitor agreed, "but the fact that Mounsey did have some chocolates will not explain his silence about his second call nor his finger-prints on the weapon."

"The latter," said Roger, "can only be accounted for by his having picked it up. Unlucky and foolish, but not incredible. Had the prints been on the butt and the trigger and not on the barrel, it would have been another matter."

A further call on Colonel Parsons showed that the old soldier's sympathies had entirely changed since his talk with Margot. But he could not go back on his story. He was ready to admit the brief interval when he had left the window, and was prepared to stress the fact that he could not see the faces of departing visitors; but that, while allowing the possibility that there had been a second caller, did nothing to prove his existence or his identity.

"I would do anything sooner than help to hang the wrong man," he roared, "but blast it! I can't unsay what I said or unsee what I saw!"

More interesting was an interview Roger had with brother Marmaduke. He did not call on Marmaduke; Marmaduke called on him.

"I want to apologise for what I said the other day," he began abruptly. "Don't know what made me do it. A bit on edge, I suppose. Devilish awkward to be under suspicion. But I am sure you will understand."

"The only thing I do not understand," Roger said, "is who made the statement that led you to come to me."

"Oh—ah—well—no use going into that now, is there? Perhaps I put two and two together and made five of it. Sorry I lost my hair. But how are things going? You are in with Scotland Yard, aren't you? What is the latest—of course in confidence?"

That, Roger thought, was the real purpose of his call. Apology was not very natural to Marmaduke, but curiosity might well be.

"How do you mean?" he asked.

"Young Mounsey's trial starts next week, doesn't it? No doubt, I suppose, that he shot Frederick?"

"Personally I think there is a good deal of doubt," said Roger.

"You do? For his sake I hope you are right. But about Alexander; no arrest yet?"

"Not yet."

"Surely they have their eye on someone?"

"On everyone," said Roger. "Isn't that what you were complaining of?"

Marmaduke stared at him, and then started again, getting perhaps closer to the reason for the call.

"It's about Helen, you know. Devilish awkward position. She cleared out of the flat, but after the funeral she went back. Seems to have enough to carry on with, but whose is it? I told you there was no will, and there isn't. Takes time to establish an intestacy, but as she wasn't his wife, she's not entitled to a bean.

"Of course I want to do the decent thing, but I've got to look after Delia's interests as well as my own."

"Is the estate a large one?" Roger asked.

"No—round about fifty thousand, as near as I can see. Alexander never went in for fancy investments; all very straightforward."

He spoke as though the amount was trivial, but he could not quite disguise his intense satisfaction.

"That would be twenty-five thousand for you, less such allowance as you made for Helen, and twenty-five thousand for Delia?"

"That's right. But if Helen was concerned in Alexander's death she wouldn't be entitled to anything, would she? I mean the law wouldn't allow it, and it would be damned wrong."

There was little doubt he hated the thought of letting Helen have anything. It would suit his book for her to be saddled with the crime. That, however, was no proof of her innocence.

"Did you know Helen pretty well?" Roger asked.

"Had to be civil to her, for Alexander's sake. Actually I couldn't bear the woman."

"Had she any particular friends?"

"Meaning men?" leered Marmaduke.

"Well—had she?"

"I wouldn't put it past her, but she was too sly to be caught."

If that were so, it was useless to pursue the subject. "Since Frederick left a will, I suppose things there are fairly simple?" Roger asked.

"Yes, quite."

"Anything to his nephew, Wilfrid Mounsey?"

"One hundred pounds."

"Perhaps it is as well it is no more."

"Wilfrid gets other money by his death," said Marmaduke pointedly.

"I know that. How is the business dealt with?"

"Everything goes to Delia. Her trustees—that is me—decide what to do with the business. At present Foyle is carrying on. He is an able fellow. I may come to terms to let him take it over. Depends of course on what happens to Wilfrid. But about Helen—"

He asked more questions concerning his reputed sister-in-law and the view the police took of her position. Roger did not gratify his curiosity.

When he had gone, Roger paid another visit to Scotland Yard; but if he had refused to give information, he was equally unable to get any. Not that Inspector Goff was unfriendly, but his enquiries had also been fruitless. He had interviewed both Helen Curtis and Evelyn Parr, and they swore their first story, was true.

"I don't believe 'em, but there it is. They stick to it that they were at the theatre together on the night of the crime. It is not easy to prove otherwise."

"You have not been able to trace any special friend of Helen Curtis?" Roger asked.

"No."

"Could Mrs. Parr explain why she saw the show twice in a few days?"

"She said a man she knew was given tickets and it was a pity to waste 'em."

"Of course you saw the man?"

"I did. I asked him if Mrs. Parr had seen the play before. He said he understood she had, though not with him."

"No doubt he had been told to say so. Her embarrassment when I spoke to her—"

"She explained that," grunted Goff. "She couldn't think who you were, yet she felt she ought to know you."

"Just girlish confusion. Did you ask the man how he got the tickets?"

"Don't think I did, but I believe they are being distributed fairly freely."

"They are," said Roger. "Mrs. Parr told you they were given to him and the manager told me they had been sold. It might be worth finding out just how he got them, though if he says he bought them, and Mrs. Parr was mistaken, it won't help us much."

Nothing just then seemed to help very much. What Dreda had told him as to Margot's reliance on his efforts did not add to his comfort. And Gordon Lisle, whom he met a little later, had to report an equal lack of success on the part of his eager young sleuths to trace Helen Curtis's supposed male friend.

"She doesn't go out much now," said the crime editor; "but she used to, quite a lot. Apparently she always started and returned alone. Often went to the Brompton Road Stores in a taxi. She is well known there, but the only person she met was her sister. Where she went from there we cannot discover. If there was any thing clandestine, she managed it very cleverly."

"I wish we could be half as clever," muttered Roger. "Two crimes, both staged to look like suicides and alike in all essential details, they must have been done by the same person. We can see people who might have done one of them, but we cannot find anyone who could have done both."

"I think that little affair outside Miss Costello's studio shows you are nearer to the solution than you realise."

Roger had, of course, told his friend of the bogus call and the attack in the dark. He had also reported it to the police. But the explanation for it had yet to be found.

"Helen's boy-friend may not help you," Lisle went on. "We want someone who played an important part in the lives of both Alexander and Frederick."

"There are two who might fill the bill," said Roger, "but both seem impossible."

"Who are they?"

"Marmaduke and Morant."

"Morant!" echoed Lisle. "The solicitor for the defence! I never thought of him. Of course he was Alexander's partner and no doubt had dealings with Frederick. What is the evidence?"

"Precious little. A lot of very pretty theory and one quite fatal objection."

"That still leaves Marmaduke. I know we considered him before, but don't forget the dictum—when you eliminate all the other possibilities what remains must be guilty, however improbable it may appear. You cannot eliminate Marmaduke. He had the opportunity, and the motive is obvious."

"Motive for killing Alexander," said Roger, "half of fifty thousand pounds. Motive for killing Frederick, some small debts but otherwise dubious. There is no doubt he was out in that car, but unless it can be shown the car was in or near Egerton Square or Sloane Avenue at the essential times you must assume his innocence. Goff knows the make and the number. It came back to the garage wet and muddy, so Marmaduke is sitting pretty."

"Except that Frederick might have had suspicions."

"To murder everyone who has suspicions would be a big order."

"It was worth trying on you," said Lisle. "But apart from Marmaduke, what put you on to the much respected Morant?"

"Has he all the money he needs? Naturally I do not know what his firm earns, but Alexander Curtis, after living a quiet life, amassed fifty thousand pounds. Victor Morant does not lead a quiet life, and fifty thousand would not go far in his activities. An expensive place in the country, where he has ambitions for Parliament. A costly flat in town, and a fondness for theatrical speculations that are not as a rule successful. A fondness, too, for his leading lady."

"You mean if he only earned what his partner earned he must have supplemented his income from other sources?"

"And where could he get it? Here is the libellous flight of imagination. He is trustee for his niece Margot's fortune; possibly for other fortunes too. Quiet-living Alexander was his partner and Frederick was the firm's accountant. Suppose there were irregularities and the partner and the accountant discovered them. If Morant removed them both he might be safe, and might, at any rate for a time, be able to carry on."

"I like this," murmured Lisle. "Any more?"

"Does not Morant's behaviour lend colour to the idea? He undertook the defence of the man accused of murdering his partner's brother. Rather an unusual thing to do, and he was at some pains to explain to me that he only did it because he was so sure of Wilfrid Mounsey's innocence. It is an appalling thing to suggest that he wants his client to hang, but has he been as energetic in the defence as he might have been?"

"You mean he was tepid about the chocolate box?"

"So much so that Gerry Bulmer asked whose side he was on. So much so that he has been insidiously preparing Margot for failure. But there are other things."

"Let us have them."

"Morant supplied the theatre tickets that got both Helen and Delia out for the night and left Alexander and Frederick at home alone. It would have been easy for him to tell the men he must see them privately. I discovered that he missed a bit of the play on the night it all happened, and that bit comes just at the time when Frederick was killed. Also there is a way by which he could have left the theatre and returned to it unobserved."

"Have you told all this to Inspector Goff?" Lisle demanded.

Roger laughed.

"Most of it," he said. "It is a castle of cards and he promptly blew it over."

"How?"

"First, there is not a scrap of proof for a single word of it. Second, Morant cannot be Helen's unknown friend, for Lotta Denys occupies too much of his time. Third, we think he is tepid about the recovery of the chocolate box because that was our own brilliant piece of work; he sees it in a different perspective, and anyway he is calling Gerry Bulmer and her boneless friend. Fourth and final, Morant never left the theatre on the night in question. Goff absolutely vouches for that, and you may take it he is right. His alibi is supported by half a dozen people, right through the evening."

For some moments Lisle was silent.

"Well," he said at last, "you had me on a piece of toast. I really thought Morant was the right answer. It only shows how one's imagination can run ahead of the facts. Failing Marmaduke and Morant—who?"

"I wish I knew," said Roger.

"Can we tackle it in any other way? You think Helen's mysterious admirer may be the link we want. Essentially a missing link. Suppose you examine the other end?"

"How do you mean?"

"The purpose of a link is to join two things together. Our link, if our theory is right, has in some way to join Helen with Frederick. Enquiry about Helen has failed. So enquire about Frederick."

"Where and how?"

"At his home. In his office."

"I am afraid the ground has been covered," said Roger. "I thought of asking if I might go through Frederick's papers, but Goff has already done so. So, later, had Morant on Mounsey's behalf. Then Marmaduke, as executor, did the like."

"What you find may depend on what you are looking for," observed Lisle sententiously.

"Helen and Frederick; I can but try. Sometimes the thing you want is staring you in the face all the time."

XXIV. LIGHT AT LAST!

ACTING on Lisle's advice, Roger's first step was to pay another visit to No. 3 Egerton Square, in the hope of seeing Delia.

"So you are still here?" he said, when she herself opened the door to him. "Uncle Marmaduke in residence?"

"Not yet. He says he will not come till after the trial."

"That is what I wanted to see you about. May I come in?" She led the way to the sitting-room where they had talked before. She was wearing a very simple black dress. It made her look more slender, and her large blue eyes and fair hair had an added beauty by contrast.

"So you are resigned to the inevitable?" he said lightly. "Uncle Marmaduke may not be so bad at close-quarters."

"Worse, I should think. Jimmie Durrant wants me to marry him."

"Are you going to?"

"I don't know."

"Not sure you love him?"

She made no answer, but Roger judged his guess was not far wrong.

"Better a few months with an uncle you dislike than a life-time with a man you do not love. If you manage Uncle Marmaduke the right way you will soon have him eating out of your hand."

"What is the right way?"

"Stand up to him. Ever worn a monocle?"

"No."

"Buy one and practise with it. It will give you confidence. When he hectors and rants, as he probably will, wait till he finishes, then fix it in your eye and say, 'Your nose is too purple. Have you seen a doctor?' Most men are sensitive about their noses. He will reply with more angry words. Let him run down and then say as coolly as before, 'Is it your heart, or are you drinking too much?'"

"I don't think I could," giggled Delia.

"It is your best chance. Never interrupt, and never reply except to make personal remarks about his health and appearance. Find out whether it is his liver or his stomach that worries him, and tell him you think it is worse! If you differ over money matters, look at him with your monocle and say, 'Very well, my good man, have it your own way now; but remember, every penny has to be accounted for when I come of age.' If you can keep that up for a week he will be trying to think of little things to please you."

"Uncle Marmaduke doing that!" she exclaimed.

"I mean it," said Roger. "He is the bully type and really a coward. I never thought I should have to teach a modern girl to be rude to her relations, but there are special cases. Now for something more serious."

"Yes?" He had quite won her over, and she would have helped him in any way she could.

"You do not believe that Wilfrid shot your father?"

"I am sure he did not. It is the most ghastly mistake. It will be all right next week, won't it?"

"I hope so," said Roger, "though I really expect a remand. Any way, since Wilfrid is innocent, can we think who did it?"

"I have tried and tried till my head was bursting, but it all seems so unreasonable and impossible. Why should anyone do such a thing to my father? He had no enemies. He was so quiet and kind"

"He was deeply interested in Biblical prophecy and that sort of thing?"

"Very, but could anything be more peaceful and innocent? He believed that the stone on which our kings are crowned in Westminster Abbey was the stone that Jacob slept on when he had the vision of the ladder to heaven. He started studying those things after my mother died. Perhaps I left him alone more than I ought to have done."

Her lips quivered. Roger remembered her self-reproaches when it was suggested that her father had shot himself.

"What I was getting at," he said quickly, "was whether this study of his brought him into contact with people who might help us if we saw them."

"I don't think so. It didn't bring him into contact with people; it kept him away from them. He used to stay in and read. There was one man he wrote to sometimes about it."

"Who was he?"

"Professor Cockington."

"Got his address?"

Delia soon found it.

"I don't see how he can help you," she said. "He only came once, about a year ago, and he hardly seemed real. The kind of man who thinks far more of a bit of ancient pottery than of clean clothes or decent food."

"I know his sort," nodded Roger, "but the world owes more to them than to those whose main concern is the comfy life. Anyone else you can think of?"

"I am afraid not. The only person who might tell you some thing is Mr. Foyle."

"I am seeing him. On what sort of terms was your father with Helen Curtis?"

"With Aunt Helen? Of course I know now she is not really my aunt; Uncle Marmaduke told me. My father really had very little to do with her."

"Are you fond of her?"

"No," said Delia frankly. "I never was. I loved Uncle Alex; he was a dear; but Aunt Helen never cared for me. I think kiddies know instinctively how the grown-ups regard them and their own feelings are affected accordingly."

Roger agreed. They chatted for some time, and when he left her she told him his call had done her a lot of good.

"Marry when you are in love," he said, "not as a means of escape. Even Uncle Marmaduke is not as bad as that. And don't forget the monocle."

He had not learned much from her and he did not expect to learn much from Professor Cockington. The professor was an elderly gentleman, bearded, very deaf, and with shaggy eyebrows that almost hid his eyes. Roger tried to explain that he was interested in Mr. Frederick Curtis who was, he believed, known to the professor as a fellow student of Biblical prophecy.

Yes, indeed, the professor remembered him, but his ideas were wrong. If he had read the last chapters of Daniel correctly and had compared them with Revelation—a mass of detail followed concerning the Number of the Beast, the promises to Jacob, Behemoth, and much else. Roger had met other old gentlemen who spent the greater part of their time wrestling with the riddles of the early Hebrews. He knew how fascinating it was, but he realised Professor Cockington was unlikely to help in his present quest. He got away as quickly as he could and hurried to Frederick Curtis's office in the City, where he was fortunate in catching Charles Foyle.

Foyle was already installed in the private room of his late employer and was obviously in control of things.

"You remember me?" said Roger.

"You were with the inspector from Scotland Yard the first time he came."

"I was with him then; now in a sense I am against him. I believe young Mounsey is innocent."

"I sincerely hope you are right," said Foyle.

"Have you any doubt of it?"

"That is not an easy question to answer. I was devoted to Mr. Curtis—all of us here were. I should never have believed Mr. Wilfrid could have injured him, but the police do not bring such terrible charges without good reason, do they? I feel we must wait for the evidence."

"How is the trial likely to affect things here?"

"If he is acquitted, it should not do us much harm. If he is not acquitted—but I hope that need not be considered."

"It is an important detail if you are buying the business, as Mr. Marmaduke gave me to understand."

"It is premature to say that," replied Foyle rather coldly. "If Mr. Wilfrid does not wish to return, I think Mr. Curtis would have liked me to carry on, to prevent the staff being discharged. Terms have been discussed, but—"

"But that is no affair of mine," supplemented Roger with a smile, as he stopped somewhat abruptly. "That is true. I came in the hope of helping Mounsey. We all believe he is innocent. Can you not suggest something that will help us to prove it?"

"In what way?"

"I realise you cannot know what happened when he called on his uncle, but if he did not shoot him, who did? I thought perhaps, knowing Mr. Curtis as you did, you could suggest some thing that might put us on the right track. It was Miss Delia's idea as well as my own."

"Mr. Bennion, if I had any such suggestion to make do you imagine I should have waited for you to come to me before making it? As I said when you were here before, I owe everything to Mr. Curtis. His death shocked me. Now, when I am told it was not suicide but murder, I am shocked, if possible, even more profoundly. If it be true, I am completely at a loss to understand it. Mr. Curtis was a man with few friends, but I should have said with no enemies. I have told all I know to the proper authorities, and I do not think any purpose will be served by my discussing it with you."

Foyle spoke with some dignity and, as he spoke, he stood up as though to suggest that the interview was over. His manner was more assured and less ingratiating than at their previous meeting.

Then the telephone bell on his table sounded.

Roger had not got up, but looked away as Foyle lifted the receiver.

"But I told you not..."

Foyle sounded angry. Then he listened again for some moments.

"I distinctly said..."

The unseen speaker evidently went on again at some length.

"I cannot talk to you now. . ."

Apparently he had to listen. He made sounds of impatience and annoyance, but the words from the other end of the wire continued.

"I am very busy. I cannot possibly..."

The one-sided conversation went on despite his obvious anger. And then—quite suddenly—Roger realised who was speaking to him. Acute as his hearing was, he could not consciously identify a word that was said. A faint buzz was occasionally audible, that was all. But some undeveloped sense told him beyond a doubt the identity of the speaker.

"Very well, very well," muttered Foyle, in something very unlike his usual suave tone, "I will be there."

"I am afraid I have taken up a lot of your time," said Roger, as the receiver was replaced. "We want to do all we possibly can for Wilfrid Mounsey, but if you cannot help us it is no good my bothering you further."

Foyle looked at him very hard before he replied. Perhaps he was wondering if the few scraps of conversation he had heard had conveyed anything to him. Then he said in his old manner:

"It is not a question of bothering me, Mr. Bennion. I would be only too glad to help you if I could. I am convinced of Mr. Wilfrid's innocence. If testimony to his character and kindly disposition would help I would gladly give it. I deeply regret I cannot do more."

Roger was relieved when he got outside, but he did not go far. It was late in the afternoon and presumably Mr. Foyle's day's work was nearly done.

He was right. Before many minutes had passed, the neatly attired accountant emerged from the door of the building of which his offices were part. He was carrying a long coat over his arm and he stepped briskly forward.

Roger followed him.

Then an odd thing happened. Foyle left the main road for a side street. He went along it for some little way without lessening his pace and stopped suddenly in a recessed doorway. He stood with his back to the street and stooped, apparently to turn up the ends of his neat striped trousers—although it was not raining. Then he slipped on his long coat.

When he turned round he was wearing a pair of big dark glasses and his felt hat was pulled well over his eyes. It was not an elaborate disguise, but no casual observer would have taken him for the same man who had just left the Curtis accountancy offices.

"Follow that cab!"

Roger saw him hail a taxi and he promptly gave chase. The drivers avoided the congestion of the City by making for the embankment. They followed the course of the river to Westminster, turned north, crossed Piccadilly Circus and reached a busy Street off Oxford Street.

The first car stopped outside the doorway of a small café. Foyle alighted, paid his driver and disappeared through the doorway. A few moments later Roger did the same.

The doorway led to a flight of stairs, the tea-room being on the first floor. It had a subdued light and the decoration was supposedly Egyptian or Turkish. The centre of the room had a few low tables, which were not in use; the sides were divided into screened recesses from which came the sounds of whispering and laughter. The attendants wore transparent gauze trousers and yashmaks.

Roger took in the nature of the place at a glance. Not necessarily vicious, but suggestive of a naughtiness that had to be paid for heavily. Curtains were draped across the recesses but did not completely enclose them. It was still possible for prying eyes to see inside.

He stepped quickly past some of the openings. Then he saw what he wanted to see—what he expected to see— and he did not think he had been seen.

"My friend is not here yet."

Certainly no friend of his! The person Charles Foyle had come to meet was Helen Curtis!

XXV. TO MEET A MURDERER

HELEN CURTIS! That sixth sense had told him the unheard voice over the telephone was hers, but it was necessary to be sure. Now he knew!

Helen Curtis and Charles Foyle! Helen's astute adviser mentioned by Alexander to Dreda was his own brother's right-hand man! Here indeed was a connecting link.

Roger could think best when walking. He left the café and made for the Park. As he tramped its less frequented pathways he tried to realise the full meaning of this astounding discovery.

That Foyle and Helen had met before, probably many times, there could be little doubt. What was the reason? Was it love? Or had Foyle known the story of Helen's matrimonial complications and had seen in them something to be turned to his own advantage?

His angry disjointed words over the telephone had not been suggestive of affection, but—Was Foyle's the hand that had killed both Alexander and Frederick Curtis?

If it were so, he might well be annoyed when Helen spoke to him and insisted on meeting him. He would realise how essential it was that their relationship should not be suspected.

And there might be another reason for his anger. By the death of Frederick he was likely to acquire a flourishing business. By the death of Alexander, Helen would become rich, and Helen was his. She did not know that Alexander had destroyed the will in her favour, and therefore Foyle did not know it. When he learned that she would have nothing, he was furious that his schemes and his crimes had so miscarried. He still had the woman! Was Helen at forty, blowsy, intemperate and penniless, an adequate reward for a man so calculating, so avaricious, so unscrupulous?

The surprises of the day were not finished. Sometimes it seems that fate, perverse and obstinate, suddenly relents and becomes prodigally kind. Roger was convinced he was on the right track at last. But many questions remained to be answered. How was Foyle's guilt to be brought home to him? Private judgment is ready enough to jump to conclusions, but the law does not work that way. There must be proof for every point before there can be a conviction.

What part in the crimes had Helen played?

He had shrunk from associating her with affairs so cold-blooded and horrible. From the first he had refused to believe that she had returned to the flat with her associate and had remained there the whole night with the murdered victim. Yet how else could it have been done? Will not an infatuated woman dare and endure almost anything at the bidding of the man she loves?

And Frederick—when was he killed? Could they be mistaken as to the time? Had the visitor who actually shot him come, not at ten o'clock, but at midnight? After his brother had met his fate and while he still awaited Delia's return?

Could admissions be wrung from Foyle and Helen separately that put together would establish the truth?

These questions and many like them were still unanswered when he reached home. As he entered his room his telephone rang. No mystery this time: Mr. Morant was speaking.

"That you, Mr. Bennion? You know we are expecting you at Ashcomb to-morrow?"

"Oh—we left it open, didn't we?"

He had never intended to go. Now it was out of the question. What excuse could he give?

"Margot will be very disappointed if you cannot come."

"I am sorry, but I cannot get away. A number of things have cropped up that I must see to."

That was true enough. He would like to see Margot, but she must wait. He did not wish at that moment to tell Morant what it was that kept him. It wanted consideration in all its bearings, and Goff and Gordon Lisle must know of it.

"It is important that you should come if you can manage it," Morant was saying. "Would it entice, you if I told you that a charming friend of yours will be with us?"

"Lotta Denys?"

"No," chuckled Morant, "not Lotta Denys and not Frank Rudway. They are otherwise engaged, and I am not sorry, as this is so much more urgent. It is Miss Dreda Costello."

"Oh!"

It might be useful to talk things over with Dreda, but she too must wait.

"I believe you introduced her to Margot," the solicitor went on, "and they seem to have become very good friends."

"I am glad."

"So am I. She will cheer Margot quite a lot in this trying time. She seems a very capable and delightful young woman. Charles Foyle is also coming."

"Foyle!" echoed Roger.

"Yes. He was Frederick Curtis's manager, you know."

"I know," said Roger.

This was indeed unexpected. The chance of seeing Foyle at close quarters and perhaps putting a few apparently innocent questions to him was another matter altogether. It was a chance not to be lost.

"But the real thing," explained Mr. Morant, "is that Sir Norman French is to drive over on Sunday afternoon. Quite unofficially, of course. But we shall hold a regular council of war to do our best for Wilfrid Mounsey next week."

"Why Foyle?" asked Roger.

"Sir Norman thinks his testimony that Wilfrid and Frederick Curtis met constantly and were on excellent terms should help us.'

"It should!"

"Then you'll come? We won't inflict any politics on you this time."

"Yes, I'll come."

"Splendid, Just one other thing. Sir Norman has heard of you and wants to see you. He says if you know anything more, or have any fresh ideas, for heaven's sake keep them to yourself until he has seen you. A lot may depend on our using them in the most effective way. Dinner time to-morrow, then."

XXVI. DINNER—AND AFTER

ONLY the five of them sat down to the meal. Mr. Morant, Margot and Dreda; Roger himself and—Charles Foyle.

How should one behave when one dines with a murderer?

That perhaps depends on the degree of one's certainty of his guilt. Perhaps, too, it depends on how the murderer behaves.

No exception could be taken to Foyle's manners. Quiet and entirely self-possessed, he was deferential to Mr. Morant and extremely polite to the girls. With his male fellow guest he was cool and guarded—or was that Roger's fancy? His only direct remark was that he had not expected to meet him again so soon.

Margot was quiet, but she had lost that terribly strained look she had worn when making her attempted "confession." Roger did not doubt that Dreda had inspired her with some of her own splendid courage.

He managed before dinner to ask about the visit to the luckless prisoner.

"He was wonderful," Margot said. "You see, he knows he is innocent and so he is sure it will all be right."

"And you told him you were sure too?"

"I did my best," answered the girl. "You still think so?"

"I do," said Roger firmly.

At table, to help her young hostess, Dreda did most of the talking, and her sense of humour and her outward serenity made things easier for everybody. No one who did not know her would have guessed at the deep ache in her own heart.

She had taken trouble with her appearance. Her hair was done in a style that suited her, and the soft tint of her blue frock made her clear, fearless eyes more blue than grey. Without her it would have been a dull party.

Yet, despite her efforts, the talk did not flow freely. Margot was thinking of her man in the prison cell. The others were conscious of her pre-occupation, or perhaps had other thoughts to engross them.

"Did Mr. Bennion tell you of the attack made on him a few nights ago outside my studio?"

Dreda had tried matters political and theatrical, now she started a more personal theme.

"He did not," said their host. "When was it? I gather you were not hurt. Was it an attempt at theft?"

"I hardly think so," replied Roger, to whom he had addressed the question. "Thieves do not wait in a cul-de-sac on the chance of a victim."

"Then how do you explain it?" asked Morant.

"Just an attempt to knock me out for a time, or for all time."

Roger spoke lightly, but he was watching Foyle.

"Why should anyone wish to knock you out?" asked that man, meeting his glance with perfect composure.

"That is what puzzles me," returned Roger.

"Were the men caught?" enquired Mr. Morant.

"No. It was all very soon over. Miss Costello opened her door and they ran away."

"Such things in the heart of London seem hardly credible," said their host warmly. "It is disgraceful. What are our police for?"

Margot said nothing. She was looking at them all with widened wondering eyes.

"Perhaps Mr. Bennion was mistaken for someone else," Foyle gently suggested.

"That is impossible," declared Dreda. "He was lured there by a false telephone message, supposed to have come from me."

"What a remarkable thing," exclaimed Mr. Morant. "But surely it ought to help to identify the parties concerned. How many people are aware that Mr. Bennion calls on you?"

"Very few," said Roger dryly, "seeing that I had only been there once before."

At that there was a pause. Roger was waiting for someone else to speak. As they did not do so, he smiled as though to turn the conversation to a less personal channel—though he still watched Foyle—and went on: "Talking of telephones, is it not remarkable how big a part they play in modern life? It is hard to believe they were unknown fifty years ago. My father tells of the days when a house in Belgravia, if it had a bathroom and the telephone, was the last word in up-to-date luxury."

"That is quite true," said Mr. Morant. "When I was a young man starting law my principals could not bring themselves to have a telephone, as there was no evidence of the identity of the speaker at the other end of the line."

"Now, I am told," remarked Foyle, and this time he was watching Roger, "there is an invention that will make every telephone a loud speaker. You press a button and everyone in the room can hear all that is said."

"Sometimes," commented Roger, "a button that prevents any one from hearing anything might be more useful."

There was another pause. Then Dreda, unconscious of any undercurrent of meaning, came again to the rescue.

"What a difference the telephone has made to the playwright. You seldom see a play without one."

"It is a new dimension," said Mr. Morant. "It makes an absent person present, and can help a lot in explaining things to the audience."

"Would Shakespeare have used it if it had been known in his day?" asked Dreda. "Can you imagine Hamlet shouting, 'Are you there?' down the telephone?"

"Or," suggested Roger, "Juliet saying to Romeo, 'Parting is such sweet sorrow, but give me a ring when you get home'?"

They laughed and for a time the chatter was frivolous and easy. When the next pause came Mr. Morant said quite suddenly—"Are you fond of moonlight bathing, Miss Costello?"

"Not in England," she replied.

"And you, Mr. Bennion?" he asked.

"Only in very hot weather," said Roger. "It sounds romantic, but is generally rather a chilly reality."

"I advise you against it," said Mr. Morant emphatically. "Our lake is alluring and some weeks ago a young friend of Margot's decided to take a midnight dip. The water was more chilly than he thought. Luckily his shouts were heard, or he might have been drowned."

"Did he go in alone?" asked Roger.

"No," said Margot. "There were four of us, but we did not miss him at first."

"The lake is deep and very cold," explained her uncle, "even on a hot night like this." He paused and went on: "Shall we have coffee on the terrace? After so much rain it is good to get a real summer night."

His suggestion was adopted. They sat on the terrace overlooking the garden which, with its mingled scent of roses, heliotropes and other plants, smelt very sweet in the still warm air. The talk was desultory. Foyle said he did not play cards. Mr. Morant suggested some music, but no one seemed keen on the idea. Drinks were brought out. Cigarettes and cigars were lit, and the moments slipped by.

"It is delightful out here," Dreda murmured. "The air is so soft."

But after a time Margot whispered to her, and they both said they would like to go to bed.

"These men have got a lot to talk about really," Margot remarked.

"And they are longing for us to go," laughed Dreda, "but are too polite to say so."

The men of course protested, but the girls wished them good-night and went in.

"There is a lot to talk about," said Mr. Morant more briskly, when they had gone. "If you will finish your drink, Mr. Bennion, we might go to my room and decide what we will say to Sir Norman French to-morrow."

How the drug was put into his drink—and by whom—Roger never knew.

They all rose when Dreda and Margot left them. His glass was on the little table at his side. When the girls had gone, he tossed off the small amount that remained in it. He was not conscious of any peculiar flavour. He turned with Foyle and Mr. Morant towards the house and they entered the host's own writing-room.

Roger realised vaguely that his feet did not seem to belong to him. They did not tread firmly on the floor. The room was moving away . . . Was he ill? . . . Had he been—?

He fell into a chair and for a long time he knew no more.

XXVII. THE PRETTIEST LITTLE PLAN

"HE is coming round. Give him another dose."

Those were the first words of which Roger was conscious; and he was not fully conscious of them.

"Let him come round. I want to talk to him."

"He can't talk with that in his mouth."

"Take it out. I will tell him that if he makes a noise you will hit him on the head. And you'll make a better job of it than those fools you sent to the studio."

"Best give him another dose."

"I tell you I want to talk to him. And if he has too much of the drug there will be a risk of it being detected."

The words were muttered in low tones, but Roger began to understand them. The stupor passed quickly. After opening his eyes, he closed them and kept them closed.

Foyle and Morant!

He had suspected Morant, but Goff gave Morant an alibi. Then he had suspected Foyle. He had come there expecting to make suspicion a certainty. He had never realised Foyle and Morant were allies, working together. . . . What a fool he had been!

He was cold. Perhaps his senses became acute because he was cold. And he was cold because he was naked. Stark naked!

He could raise his eyelids, but there was little else he could raise. He was tied in a sort of invalid chair. Each leg was fastened, and each arm. There were cords round his waist and his neck, knotted to the iron framework at the back. A handkerchief stuffed into his mouth prevented his uttering a sound and added greatly to his discomfort.

He was still in Morant's writing-room. . . . Why had they urged him to come there that night? . . . For what reason had he been drugged and his clothes removed?

"Let us do it and get it over."

Foyle muttered that.

"Don't be a fool. It is too early. There might be someone about."

That was Morant's reply.

As he spoke, Morant turned the chair. It was on wheels and moved easily. He turned it till the helpless victim it carried faced more directly the bright light of a lamp on the desk.

Roger opened his eyes. His brain was alert— sufficiently alert for him to be able to disguise the fact.

"Well, Mr. Bennion," said Morant mockingly, and despite his silver hair and his kindly expression there was the light of untold cruelty in his eyes, "you see now how foolish it is not to take warnings when friends are kind enough to send them. You were told to discontinue your misguided inquiries into the Curtis affairs. Did you act on that advice? You did not. Then you had an even more forcible hint. As you informed us to-night, two men tried to knock you out for a time, or for all time. They failed, but did you take to heart the very obvious lesson? Again you did not. So if the result is regrettable, there is only yourself to blame. I hope you appreciate that?"

Roger did not reply, for the simple reason that reply was impossible. And it is poor fun to bait a victim who cannot answer back.

"I am going to remove your gag," Morant went on softly, "because I want to have a chat with you. But remember, if you raise your voice a pitch higher than mine, Foyle will hit you with that poker. I hate violence, but I am sure you understand the position."

As he spoke he removed the handkerchief. "Now drink this."

He held a glass to Roger's lips. Roger shook his head.

"Don't be afraid. It is quite harmless this time. I will take some myself."

He did so. Then, with his mocking smile, he offered it again to his victim. Roger drank. The relief was immediate.

"I want you to tell me what you know."

"I know," said Roger very slowly and very quietly, "I know that you and Foyle murdered Alexander and Frederick Curtis."

"Really? Do you know anything else?"

"Foyle did the shooting. You let him out of the theatre and you let him in again through the goods doorway."

"That is very clever of you. Now I want you to tell me how you got to know of it."

Morant spoke as coolly as before, though the dangerous glint in his eye was more evident. He could not tell that Roger was in part guessing, in part verifying his suspicions. Perhaps it made little difference.

Roger did not reply. He realised the hopelessness of his position. These two desperate men had him at their mercy and did not mean to let him get away alive. Was there a chance? He could not see a glimmer. . . except that it might be well to keep Morant uncertain.

The house was in silence. The only sound was the ticking of a clock on the mantelpiece. Its hands pointed to a quarter past one. It was not much after ten when Dreda and Margot left them. Now everyone was asleep— everyone except himself and these two men who had decided on his destruction.

Foyle had not spoken again. Roger could just see him, a little behind the chair, standing in menacing silence with the poker in his hand.

"I want to know how you became so wise?"

As he repeated his question Morant raised a pointing finger and came a step nearer.

Still Roger did not answer.

"You won't tell me? Then shall I tell you? You have been an interfering fool, Bennion, from the start; and interfering fools deserve all they get. But for you it would have been assumed that both Alexander and Frederick Curtis committed suicide. Your friend, Inspector Goff, was not so very bright, was he?"

"Do you imagine that Goff was satisfied that the two brothers committed suicide on the same night, at the same time, and for no real reason?"

Loyalty compelled the disclaimer.

"Possibly not," said Moran; "but the reason might have been forthcoming."

"You yourself admitted there was none."

"And you," retorted Moran; "spoiled one of the prettiest little plans ever devised."

Roger tried to look sceptical. He knew there were men, especially men of a criminal turn of mind, who loved to brag of their cleverness. Morant might be one of them. The only chance was to keep him talking.

He soon began.

"If Alexander Curtis had been helping himself to his clients' money, and Frederick Curtis, the accountant brother, had been aiding him to do it, there might come a time when discovery was inevitable. Then suicide would be the only way out. Don't you agree?"

He smiled with diabolical satisfaction. Roger stared at him; everything was becoming clear.

"Yes," he said slowly. "Suicide might be the only way out—or murder, if the real thieves wished to put the shame of their wrong doing on innocent men."

"How quick you are," jeered Moran; "when someone tells you all about it!"

"I suppose it is Margot's money."

"Then you are simpler than I thought. Margot's money is intact. All my clients' moneys are intact. It is Alexander's clients who have suffered. It took a bit of managing, but when we went to the police with the sad story of what we had discovered, investigations would be inevitable and I should have to show my slate was clean. We chose our victims carefully, I assure you."

Roger said nothing. This callous avowal of crime might mean many things. But one thing was outstanding. He would never be allowed the chance of repeating it.

"Had the suicide idea been held for only three or four days," Morant went on, "we should have told our unhappy story, and no one after that would have questioned it. Of course the double suicide seemed strange, but there was the motive! We had to give ourselves a little time to discover it, but you—damn, blast and rot you!—you spoilt it."

He broke off with an angry snarl unlike his previous complacent jeering manner.

"Yes," said Roger, "the reasons for suicides would not look so good when they were found to be murders. But if your pretty plan was spoilt, it was because it was not so clever as you thought."

"Nor so clever as you think yourself," Morant retorted. "You are clever, aren't you? You got that fool Colonel Parsons to change his tone. You traced the chocolate box. You found the newsagent who thought he saw someone call at 3 Egerton Square. You met Mrs. Parr at the theatre and guessed she had not been with Helen Curtis on the night Alexander died. You bet Frank Rudway he could not leave and return to the theatre unseen. Very cunning, but the simple idiot told me about it. You followed Foyle to the tea-room when he met Helen Curtis. He saw you, though you didn't know it. Oh, yes, you are clever. How much of this have you told Inspector Goff?"

The question was shot out suddenly at the end of the tirade and Roger realised it was the clue to the whole conversation. Morant was not bragging of his own smartness without a purpose. He was not setting out Roger's discoveries for the sake of talking. He wanted to know, he wanted to know desperately badly, just how much Inspector Goff had been told; just what he and Foyle were up against. In his telephone invitation he had said that Sir Norman French, coming on Sunday, had asked that all facts and ideas should be kept secret until they met. That telephone invitation must have been made directly Foyle reported that he had been followed. Sir Norman's visit was probably a myth. Did Goff know that Foyle was the friend behind Helen Curtis? That was what Morant was so anxious to find out!

"Do you mean," said Roger, purposely missing the point, "that you would have suppressed the things I discovered, if you could, and would have let Wilfrid Mounsey hang for what you had done?"

Morant gave a short laugh.

"If Goff makes mistakes that is his affair. What did you tell him?"

"Will you inform me why you removed my clothes?"

A natural question, though irrelevant at the moment. Roger was still considering what it was wisest to say about Goff.

Morant's evil eyes glittered. Perhaps he did enjoy bragging.

"Really, Bennion," he jeered, "I thought you had intelligence enough to guess a simple thing like that! Do you not remember our discussing moonlight bathing at dinner? Did I not try to persuade you not to do it? Margot and your dear friend, Miss Costello, will recollect that I did. So will the butler and the maid. When your body is found in the water some time to-morrow, your dressing-gown and pyjamas on the bank and your clothes in the bedroom, it will be seen that the temptation was too much for you. The effect, no doubt, of so warm a night after many cooler ones. I am sorry if your nakedness shocks your modesty, but it is not our fault that you did not bring a bathing suit, is it? And in moonlight bathing hot-headed youth likes to get back to nature. Drowning, I am told, is a pleasant death. But you will not know much about it. You will just pass away in your sleep! I hope you appreciate the forethought of the wheeled chair? It is an awkward job to carry a man to the water. But in that chair it is swift, easy and silent! I know you did not tell Goff about that meeting in the tea room, so it is useless to pretend you did. You were watched."

He was far less sure than he professed to be, but Roger hardly heard his last words. He had known he was facing death. He had faced it before, and he was no coward. But the callous devilry of Morant's intentions and his own helplessness to fight them struck a new chill to his heart.

"Let me tell you," he tried to speak boldly. "Let me tell you that both Inspector Goff and Gordon Lisle know what I know. There is such a thing as a telephone. We discussed that too at dinner!"

"You swear you telephoned them?"

"Why should I swear it? You would not believe it any better."

"You shall tell me just what you told them."

"I will not."

"Oh, yes, you will! There are ways of making people talk! A burning match to the arm—or perhaps to the feet—"

"Which will hardly support the idea of accidental drowning," Roger retorted. "If anything happens to me here, do you think you will get away with it? They know what I am after—"

"And they will be able to prove precisely nothing," cut in Morant. "So foolish to bathe by moonlight when you have been warned!"

"What is the use of talking?" growled Foyle, speaking for the first time. "You have said too much already. We must get rid of him. We can take care of ourselves."

"You are right. Go ahead!"

Morant snapped the order. Foyle stepped back, but there was no crashing blow with his poker. Roger braced himself for an effort. . . for a shout. He felt a sudden prick in his neck, where the dark hair would hide any small mark.

He knew what it meant. In a few seconds the hypodermic needle would do its deadly work.

He shouted!

Before the sound could leave his lips, Morant sprang at him and thrust a muffler over his mouth. His head sank forward. Helpless, unconscious. Those who thought only of the safety of their foul selves could do with him as they liked.

XXVIII. THE LAKE

WITHOUT a sound the chair left the sleeping house. Swiftly, noiselessly, with its inert burden hidden in a dark rug, it was pushed from the silent hall, along the deserted pathways, across a lawn, down to the edge of the lake.

A still night, well suited to the awful purpose of ruthless men ready to take another life to cover the crimes they had already committed.

The waters, fringed with tall trees and hanging bushes, looked grim and forbidding. A small boat was tied to the wooden staging in front of the bathing hut. To free the body in the chair from the cords that held it, and to lift it into the boat, was the work of a very few moments.

To push off, and with three or four strokes of the oars to reach the centre of the lake, did not take so long.

To hoist the body overboard without upsetting the frail craft was less easy. But it was soon done. With little more than a ripple, the stark white form slid into the deepest stretch of the sombre pool.

A few more strokes brought the boat to land. Some clothes were deposited on the step of the hut and, without a backward glance, those who had accomplished their foul deed made their hurried return to the house to fortify themselves with strong drink and to seek their guilty pillows.

But—had they waited—had they been less hurried—had they given a backward glance—they might have seen a new ripple in the water.

On the farther side of the little lake something already immersed began to move. Had it been seen, it might have been taken for a shadow or a piece of floating wood. Under the fringe of a willow it was not seen at all.

It moved at first slowly and then more rapidly. A human form in a black bathing suit with long black gloves and a black head covering. Nearing the centre of the water, it dived. The white, motionless body was brought to the surface, and, with a skill that told of courage and training, was borne to the willow-sheltered shallow, where other arms were stretched out to drag it to land.

"What has happened?"

Roger Bennion opened his eyes, but his mind was still in some far-off, unhappy dream. Wrapped in rugs and with a flask of brandy at his lips, returning warmth brought consciousness. Yet he knew nothing of the artificial respiration, or of the vigorous rubbing that had restored something of the glow of animation to his chilled body. At first he could not even recognise the shadowy forms that bent over him.

"Are you all right?"

He knew the voice. It was Dreda's. And the other kindly being still chafing his hands was Margot.

"I am all right. What has happened?"

As he repeated the question, recollection returned. It had been no purpose of those who meant to drown him to mark his body or to give him more of the drug than was sufficient for their aim. The chill of the water and the prompt aid of his rescuers restored his senses remarkably quickly.

"Never mind that now," said Dreda. "We have a car close by and we must get away at once if you can manage it."

"I am all right. Have I any clothes?"

He sat up as he spoke, and he knew the answer to the question. "Never mind clothes," said Dreda. "The rugs will do. Can you get up?"

She had removed her own bathing things and was wearing a warm coat and skirt. Margot was also dressed for travel. He rose to his feet, with the rug wrapped round him, and with the aid of the girls, he staggered to the car. He got in and another rug was produced.

"Where shall we go?" asked Margot.

"You know what it means?"

"I do," she said.

"Go to Scotland Yard as quickly as you can."

"I will drive. You look after him, Dreda, and tell him about it." It was Dreda's car, but Margot took the wheel. She drove down a side path, keeping well away from the house, and in a few moments they were through the gates, on the road, heading for London.

"Have some more." Dreda handed him the flask.

He took it, and the generous warmth of the spirit was like new life to him. In a stronger voice he said: "Tell me how the miracle happened."

"No miracle," Dreda replied. "It is thanks to Margot, and is all quite simple. She supposed you and Mr. Foyle and her uncle were going to discuss what was best for Wilfrid. She was desperately anxious to hear what you really thought, so she went into the garden to listen. The window was not quite shut. You can imagine her horror when she realised that it was her uncle and Foyle who had murdered Alexander and Frederick, and that they had no intention of saving Wilfrid. And they meant to drown you to prevent your doing so. She came and told me."

"And you?"

"I did not know what to do. I could hardly believe it at first. Margot was almost hysterical at her uncle's wickedness. She wanted us to go for the police, but I was afraid we might not be back in time. The telephone was in the room where you were; we could not use that. We thought of going in and saying what we knew. But we were afraid. They were desperate and there might have been three bathing accidents, not one! Then we decided if we could rescue you that would be best. You knew everything and would see justice done."

"You got to the lake before they did?"

"Yes. We managed to get the car out without making too much noise. Luckily the garage is a little way from the house. We took rugs and things, and I am a pretty good swimmer. There was one horrible thought."

"What was that?" Roger asked.

"I saw their game. They did not want to injure you in any way; it had to be an accident while swimming. Cramp, or something like that."

"Yes?"

"My fear was that they would hold you under."

"Not a nice idea at all," said Roger. "I almost wonder they didn't!"

"Had there been any sign of it, we meant to appear on the bank and shout. They could hardly have done it while we were watching, and Margot would have gone off in the car for help. That was our second plan. But, at it was, they were in too great a hurry to get away."

"You were wonderful," Roger murmured, "both of you. I can never hope to repay you."

"Save Wilfrid, that is all Margot asks."

"And you?"

"If the men who murdered Alexander get what they deserve—do you not think that will satisfy me?"

He had never before heard her speak with such passion.

"They shall," he whispered.

Mr. Morant and Charles Foyle were down in good time for breakfast the next morning. Mr. Morant appeared more benign than ever. His silver hair shone brightly and his fresh colour was a picture of health and good nature. Foyle looked pale. Perhaps he had not slept so well.

"Margot and Miss Costello are late," Morant remarked. "We will not wait. I feel hungry."

Foyle did not reply. He helped himself to eggs and bacon.

"Make a good meal," said his host. "There is nothing to worry about. Just remember to be natural."

Still Foyle said nothing.

"Glad it is such a fine day. I suppose you are not coming to church with me?"

Before Foyle could reply—if he would have replied—a noise outside was heard.

"They have found the body," Morant whispered, "and have come to bring us the sad news. Poor Mr. Bennion! He was such an amusing person! Take some more coffee and see that your hand is steady!"

The door opened. But it was not one of the servants who entered. It was Chief-Inspector Goff and two of his assistants.

"Victor Morant and Charles Foyle, I arrest you both for the murder of Alexander and Frederick Curtis."

As he spoke his assistants did their part. Handcuffs were snapped on the wrists of the astonished men. They might have protested, but, before the words could come, Roger Bennion appeared in the doorway.

Then they had nothing to say.

XXIX. PUNISHMENT AND REWARDS

"IT has always been my view," said Sir Christopher, "that what we call coincidences are generally the normal working of natural laws. We now find that the strange coincidence of the suicide of the two brothers was neither suicide nor coincidence. It was just a devilishly clever scheme of murder."

"Was it so clever?" asked Gordon Lisle. "If success be the measure of cleverness, this was a sorry piece of bungling. What do you say, Goff?"

"I agree with Sir Christopher," replied the inspector. "It was devilishly clever, but the devil seldom wins in the end. Now we have the whole story, we can see how ingenious it was."

"Is there anything fresh?" Roger enquired.

Once again the four of them had dined in his flat, and after a satisfying repast had resumed their discussion almost where they left it off about three weeks before. It was a few days after the arrest. Foyle and Morant had been formally charged and Wilfrid Mounsey had been released. Roger had suggested the little party, and Goff had agreed. Lisle saw many scoops for his journal, and Sir Christopher was only too pleased to meet them all again, to talk over the case that was the sensation of the hour.

"There is not really much more than you told me," Goff said in reply to Roger's question. "Just a little straightening out of the details. Morant sees the game is up, so he wants to turn King's evidence."

"What a man!" cried Roger. "He indeed likes to play many parts. Lawyer, politician, theatrical magnate; now it is first conspirator, solicitor for the defence, and chief witness! I suppose he wants to throw the blame on Foyle?"

"That's it. He says the original misdoing was a slip on his part, not a deliberate theft. Foyle detected it and suggested ways in which it could be covered up and other sums taken. Morant and Curtis, the solicitors, handle many trust funds, and Frederick Curtis, the accountant, certified things for them. Frederick trusted Foyle implicitly and left most of the work to him. So Morant and Foyle, working together, were able to help themselves freely with very little risk of detection."

"Foyle must have put away a tidy bit," remarked Lisle. "He lived in his old simple way."

"For a man earning a few hundreds a year to start buying costly cars and a country house would have looked suspicious," Roger commented. "I think Foyle realised that."

"Foyle was waiting his time," said Goff, "but Morant grew more extravagant. He took Ashcomb, he wanted to stand for Parliament, and, as you just mentioned, he dabbled in theatrical speculations. This meant dipping so heavily into the trust funds that at last the suspicions of both the Curtis brothers were aroused. Investigations would, of course, have exposed and ruined Foyle as well as Morant. It was then, according to Morant, that Foyle suggested that the accounts should be manipulated so that it would appear that the frauds had been carried out by Alexander in collusion with Frederick—just as in fact he and Morant had really been acting."

"And that necessitated the murder of the brothers," commented Sir Christopher.

"Exactly, sir. Foyle and Morant prepared duplicate books and everything was ready. Had the double suicide been accepted for only a few days, however strange it appeared, they would have come to us with their stories. They had not been quite happy about things, but Morant trusted Curtis, and it was not for Foyle to accuse his employer. Now they had looked into affairs and were horrified at what they found. That would have been their line. The brothers had evidently realised it could not go on, so suicide had been their way out."

"Do you think you would have accepted that idea?" asked the baronet.

"Luckily, sir," replied Goff dryly, "the question does not arise. Thanks to your son, the suicide myth was at once disposed of, and so their plan, clever as it was, miscarried. Later on, no doubt, they would still have tried to throw the blame for the missing funds on the dead men, but it was too dangerous to bring forward a story to account for suicides when it was known the suicides were murders!"

"Just how were the murders carried out?" asked Lisle.

"Pretty much as Mr. Bennion described. Morant made an appointment with each of the brothers separately to call round in the evening with Foyle to explain matters. He provided theatre tickets so that they might send out the women-folk and be at home alone."

"Alexander told Dreda Costello he was expecting a visitor on important business," Roger remarked. "In the circumstances he could not explain what it was."

"When Foyle arrived, he was to suggest they should wait for Morant. He was then to take the earliest chance of shooting his victim. This was to happen in each case."

"That is Morant's story?" asked Roger.

"Yes. He says he protested, but was over-persuaded."

"Personally I should say his was the master-mind. He took care about his own alibi, and as Foyle did the actual shooting, Morant will put on him all the blame he can. Did he say anything more?"

"Foyle was to make it appear the deaths happened just before eleven, and was to get back to the theatre as quickly as he could."

"Did he admit he had let Foyle out by the back way," Roger asked, "and had let him in again?"

"He did."

"Then I cannot see that one of them is more guilty than the other. I hope they both hang. What about Helen Curtis? Was she a party to the death of Alexander?"

"I have seen her," Goff replied, "and I think she is too scared to keep anything back. She had been told nothing, and went home as she described. When she heard the news in the morning, she really thought Alexander had shot himself."

"But she knew Foyle had left her during the evening," said Roger.

"He told her he had to go out on business. At first, at any rate, she did not suspect what business! Alexander's death was intended to appear as suicide, and, if she thought that, they judged she would act more naturally than if she had to play a part. They were right up to a point, but their precaution in that way led her to err in another."

"You mean as to her companion?" suggested Roger.

"Yes. They intended her to supply Foyle's alibi, should it be needed. He was furious when he knew she said she was with her sister; but, of course, it was his own fault."

"How long had the affair with Foyle been going on?"

"For quite a considerable time," said Goff, "and the sister had always been the cloak. When I asked who was with her that night, Helen did not know the special reason for saying it was Foyle, and stuck to the old lie."

"Was Foyle really keen on her?" inquired Lisle. "How did it start?"

"I have no precise information," Goff replied.

"My theory," said Roger, "is that she welcomed Foyle's attentions, and told him how things were between herself and her supposed husband, who wanted to marry Dreda Costello. Foyle saw a chance of squeezing a fat settlement which would make Helen highly desirable. That was the position before the frauds by Morant and himself were suspected. Then murder was decided on. Foyle believed the old will stood, but he cannot have expected much from it."

"Fifty thousand!" said Lisle.

"He knew better than that. He and Morant were putting their frauds on to Alexander, so Alexander's private estate would vanish. Foyle had gone too far with Helen to dare to quarrel with her, but he was not very amiable about it, quite apart from her error over the alibi."

"The great thing for both Foyle and Morant," said Goff, "was that their misdoings were wiped out."

"I agree," nodded Roger. "In addition to that, Foyle was left in peaceable possession of the thousands he had stolen, and he no doubt counted on getting Frederick's business."

"And Morant?" asked Lisle.

"Morant told me he had selected his victims carefully," replied Roger. "That no doubt means the defaults would as far as possible have been made personal to Alexander. Morant got a clean slate and the chance to start again!"

"I suppose his talk of capital levy," said Goff, "was just eyewash."

"Why eye-wash?" asked Roger. "He practised what he preached!"

"But not for the common weal," said Sir Christopher. "Murder is always terrible, but it is most dastardly when its purpose is to sully the names and memories of its victims with frauds of which they were innocent. That was the purpose of Morant and Foyle, and it is indeed a matter for thankfulness, Inspector Goff, that you have exposed them and brought them to justice."

"The credit, Sir Christopher," replied Goff, "is due mainly to your son. I was not very happy about the arrest of Wilfrid Mounsey, and when the chocolate box turned up I was pretty sure a mistake had been made. We had no reasons for suspecting Morant, and his alibi was cast-iron. What we really missed was his connection with Foyle."

"I missed that too," said Roger. "Otherwise I would not have paid my second visit to Ashcomb with its risks of moonlight bathing! But if we are handing out bouquets, we must not forget Lisle and his lads."

"I was waiting for that kind word," said the crime editor, "although it is contrary to our custom to take credit to ourselves."

"I am sure it is," said Roger, raising his glass. "Let us drink to Modesty, Justice, and the enterprise of the British Press!"

Two days later a very small party gathered at one of the lesser known West End churches for a very quiet wedding. Margot had begged that no one should be told of it, for she knew that, with Wilfrid's release and her uncle's arrest, it would attract more attention than they wished. Marmaduke Curtis was to give the bride away and Delia was her sole attendant. Jimmie Durrant was the best man.

Gordon Lisle was there. It would be another wonderful scoop for his paper at the week-end, but till then not a word was to be whispered.

Roger arrived in good time and he met Dreda in the porch. She greeted him with her usual serene smile. "I hear you are to be congratulated on another success," she said.

"What is that?"

"Delia is standing up to Uncle Marmaduke and is winning all along the line!"

"Splendid! But there is still something that worries me."

"Can I help?"

"I hope so," said Roger. "How am I to thank you for what you did for me? You saved my life, and words are so feeble."

"You do not think you have to offer to marry me?" she said in pretended alarm.

"Would that be a reward or a punishment?" he asked,

"Neither is needed. I loved Alexander. I doubt if I shall love anyone else. But if you would like me to paint your portrait—?"

"Unless you think I would be a model in marble? You had an opportunity of judging!"

"Hush!" she said. "Here they are?"

Wilfrid was waiting inside the church. He had arrived in a taxi. Now a car drew up. It had on it the luggage with which the happy pair were to drive away, for there was to be no festive farewell.

Marmaduke got out and gallantly escorted the bride up the aisle. Margot, though plainly dressed, looked happy and really beautiful.

The simple ceremony was over, and the good-byes were at the church door. Last of all Margot kissed Roger.

"We can never thank you enough," she whispered.

Then, as she got into the car, they heard Wilfrid say: "I am frightfully sorry, darling. I had a lovely box of chocolates for you, but I left them in the taxi!"

THE END

Other Resurrected Press Books in *The Chief Inspector Pointer Mystery* Series

Murder at Bridge

When an afternoon bridge party attended by some of Hamilton's leading citizens ends with the hostess being murdered in her boudoir, Special Investigator Dundee of the District Attorney's office is called in. But one of the attendees is guilty? There are plenty of suspects: the victim's former lover, her current suitor, the retired judge who is being blackmailed, the victim's maid who had been horribly disfigured accidentally by the murdered woman, or any of the women who's husbands had flirted with the victim. Or was she murdered by an outsider whose motive had nothing to do with the town of Hamilton. Find the answer in... **Murder at Bridge**

One Drop of Blood

When Dr. Koenig, head of Mayfield Sanitarium is murdered, the District Attorney's Special Investigator, "Bonnie" Dundee must go undercover to find the killer. Were any of the inmates of the asylum insane enough to have committed the crime? Or, was it one of the staff, motivated by jealousy? And what was is the secret in the murdered man's past. Find the answer in... **One Drop of Blood**

AVAILABLE FROM RESURRECTED PRESS!

THE EDWARDIAN DETECTIVES
LITERARY SLEUTHS OF THE EDWARDIAN ERA

The exploits of the great Victorian Detectives, Poe's C. Auguste Dupin, Gaboriau's Lecoq, and most famously, Arthur Conan Doyle's Sherlock Holmes, are well known. But what of those fictional detectives that came after, those of the Edwardian Age? The period between the death of Queen Victoria and the First World War had been called the Golden Age of the detective short story, but how familiar is the modern reader with the sleuths of this era? And such an extraordinary group they were, including in their numbers an unassuming English priest, a blind man, a master of disguises, a lecturer in medical jurisprudence, a noble woman working for Scotland Yard, and a savant so brilliant he was known as "The Thinking Machine."

To introduce readers to these detectives, Resurrected Press has assembled a collection of stories featuring these and other remarkable sleuths in The Edwardian Detectives.

- The Case of Laker, Absconded by Arthur Morrison
- The Fenchurch Street Mystery by Baroness Orczy
- The Crime of the French Café by Nick Carter
- The Man with Nailed Shoes by R Austin Freeman
- The Blue Cross by G. K. Chesterton
- The Case of the Pocket Diary Found in the Snow by Augusta Groner
- The Ninescore Mystery by Baroness Orczy
- The Riddle of the Ninth Finger by Thomas W. Hanshew
- The Knight's Cross Signal Problem by Ernest Bramah

- The Problem of Cell 13 by Jacques Futrelle
- The Conundrum of the Golf Links by Percy James Brebner
- The Silkworms of Florence by Clifford Ashdown
- The Gateway of the Monster by William Hope Hodgson
- The Affair at the Semiramis Hotel by A. E. W. Mason
- The Affair of the Avalanche Bicycle & Tyre Co., LTD by Arthur Morrison

RESURRECTED PRESS CLASSIC
MYSTERY CATALOGUE

Journeys into Mystery
Travel and Mystery in a More Elegant Time

The Edwardian Detectives
Literary Sleuths of the Edwardian Era

Gems of Mystery
Lost Jewels from a More Elegant Age

E. C. Bentley
Trent's Last Case: The Woman in Black

Ernest Bramah
Max Carrados Resurrected:
The Detective Stories of Max Carrados

Agatha Christie
The Secret Adversary
The Mysterious Affair at Styles

Octavus Roy Cohen
Midnight

Freeman Wills Croft
The Ponson Case
The Pit Prop Syndicate

J. S. Fletcher
The Herapath Property
The Rayner-Slade Amalgamation
The Chestermarke Instinct
The Paradise Mystery
Dead Men's Money

The Middle of Things
Ravensdene Court
Scarhaven Keep
The Orange-Yellow Diamond
The Middle Temple Murder
The Tallyrand Maxim
The Borough Treasurer
In the Mayor's Parlour
The Saftey Pin

R. Austin Freeman
*The Mystery of 31 New Inn from the Dr. Thorndyke
Series*
*John Thorndyke's Cases from the Dr. Thorndyke
Series*
The Red Thumb Mark from The Dr. Thorndyke Series
The Eye of Osiris from The Dr. Thorndyke Series
A Silent Witness from the Dr. John Thorndyke Series
The Cat's Eye from the Dr. John Thorndyke Series
*Helen Vardon's Confession: A Dr. John Thorndyke
Story*
As a Thief in the Night: A Dr. John Thorndyke Story
*Mr. Pottermack's Oversight: A Dr. John Thorndyke
Story*
*Dr. Thorndyke Intervenes: A Dr. John Thorndyke
Story*
The Singing Bone: The Adventures of Dr. Thorndyke
The Stoneware Monkey: A Dr. John Thorndyke Story
*The Great Portrait Mystery, and Other Stories: A
Collection of Dr. John Thorndyke and Other Stories*
The Penrose Mystery: A Dr. John Thorndyke Story
The Uttermost Farthing: A Savant's Vendetta

Arthur Griffiths
The Passenger From Calais
The Rome Express

Louis Tracy
The Strange Case of Mortimer Fenley
The Albert Gate Mystery
The Bartlett Mystery
The Postmaster's Daughter
The House of Peril
The Sandling Case: What Would You Have Done?
Charles Edmonds Walk
The Paternoster Ruby

John R. Watson
The Mystery of the Downs
The Hampstead Mystery

Edgar Wallace
The Daffodil Mystery
The Crimson Circle

Carolyn Wells
Vicky Van
The Man Who Fell Through the Earth
In the Onyx Lobby
Raspberry Jam
The Clue
The Room with the Tassels
The Vanishing of Betty Varian
The Mystery Girl
The White Alley
The Curved Blades
Anybody but Anne
The Bride of a Moment
Faulkner's Folly
The Diamond Pin
The Gold Bag
The Mystery of the Sycamore
The Come Backy

Raoul Whitfield
Death in a Bowl

And much more!
Visit ResurrectedPress.com
for our complete catalogue

About Resurrected Press

A division of Intrepid Ink, LLC, Resurrected Press is dedicated to bringing high quality, vintage books back into publication. See our entire catalogue and find out more at www.ResurrectedPress.com.

About Intrepid Ink, LLC

Intrepid Ink, LLC provides full publishing services to authors of fiction and non-fiction books, eBooks and websites. From editing to formatting, from publishing to marketing, Intrepid Ink gets your creative works into the hands of the people who want to read them. Find out more at www.IntrepidInk.com.

CPSIA information can be obtained
at www.ICGtesting.com
Printed in the USA
BVHW040826130420
577476BV00008B/84

9 781943 403295